The Tormented One

Vicki Lucky

Bloomington, IN  Milton Keynes, UK

authorHOUSE®

AuthorHouse™
1663 Liberty Drive, Suite 200
Bloomington, IN 47403
www.authorhouse.com
Phone: 1-800-839-8640

AuthorHouse™ *UK Ltd.*
500 Avebury Boulevard
Central Milton Keynes, MK9 2BE
www.authorhouse.co.uk
Phone: 08001974150

First published by AuthorHouse 5/22/2007

ISBN: 978-1-4343-0555-8 (sc)

Library of Congress Control Number: 2007903269

Printed in the United States of America
Bloomington, Indiana

This book is printed on acid-free paper.

In loving memory

of my sister, Tina,

whose never-ending strength

and courage

will inspire me always.

CHAPTER 1

It began as a typical day in the life of Detective Gina Perry. An attractive young woman with shoulder length brown hair, blue eyes, and an understanding smile, her demeanor could change abruptly from soft-spoken to a strong woman carrying the weight of the world on her narrow shoulders. Police work had brought her out of her shell and she thrived in a workplace dominated by men. Many said she would not make it through the Academy, that the arduous physical exertion would be overwhelming. But she struggled through in pursuit of her dream of becoming a detective.

As she walked up the courthouse steps, she tried to gather herself for the courtroom. She was to testify once again as one of the detectives on a brutal homicide case. Although she told others that it didn't bother her in the least, only she knew the truth. Testifying made her extremely nervous. On the prior evening, she had been awake most of the night reliving the events of the case over and over in her mind. But she had it together. No one would sense her fears. Especially not today.

Gina waited patiently for court to begin. The bailiff finally asked everyone in the courtroom to please rise for the Honorable Judge William Slocum. Gina was the first witness to testify and bristled with anticipation when her name was called.

As she walked towards the witness stand, she was the epitome of a woman in command. Dressed in a conservative blue suit and wearing very little makeup, Gina exchanged glances with Judge Slocum as she sat in the witness chair. He was a well-known and powerful man, who had made many controversial decisions, despite being one of the youngest judges in the city. This only worsened the nausea in her stomach. Although she had testified in Judge Slocum's courtroom several times before, she remained intimidated. He rarely cracked a smile and was not a very personable man.

Gina reluctantly stated her full name for the record: Gina Cassandra Perry. She had never cared for her middle name; it seemed too formal for her personality. She answered the prosecuting attorney's questions, almost answering each question before it was asked.

She found herself surviving cross-examination by the defense attorney with relative ease, thwarting every attempt to create reasonable doubt in the minds of the jurors.

The defendant, Dwayne Timbers, had been involved in an argument with his girlfriend. The two had fought frequently, but this time he had beaten her to death with a hammer. The girl was barely recognizable even to relatives.

Timbers stared coldly into the fearful eyes of every jury member, as well as Detective Perry's. His sinister eyes and calculating grin seemed to challenge her to continue, which she did undauntedly. She had faced others like him; he was not special!

After a further barrage of questioning, she was excused by Judge Slocum. Gina marched proudly down the courtroom aisle, knowing that she had played a significant role in the criminal justice system and more importantly, in the life of Timbers. She had always been an idealist and this had only added to the joking by her cohorts in the department.

Cases like this gave her life great meaning. Highly involved in her career, it had taken its toll by leaving a debris of relationships in its path. She could never seem to balance her time evenly and the men always wanted to come first, regardless of the severity of her caseload.

Gina left the courthouse in an uproar. Attorneys, police officers, witnesses, and courtroom observers were smiling deliriously and talking feverishly of how she had single handedly sealed the case. She provided the reporters with no comments and walked quickly to her police vehicle, an unmarked dark blue Chevy.

She drove to the police department and was greeted pleasantly by the other detectives in the squad. Her partner, Bob Wilson, gave her a big hug and said, "Congratulations, Perry." Bob then jokingly asked, "Did you leave anything for me to tell the jury?" This was quite a turnaround from the way he had treated her when she first made detective four years ago. Bob had even expressed his dissatisfaction to Chief Buchanon when she was assigned as his partner. Bob was a huge man, about 6'4", 280 pounds, with a handshake capable of breaking bones. But, over the years he had become more like a big teddy bear to Gina. She had proven herself way beyond what would have been required of a male partner. Bob had grown to accept her and they worked well together most of the time.

At her desk, she found a magnificent bouquet of red and yellow roses. She immediately knew who had sent them. It was the trademark of Derick Richards, her most recent boyfriend. They had dated off and on until three weeks ago when they mutually decided to end the relationship. Derick felt he wasn't good enough for Gina and that she deserved a more educated man. A construction worker, he had never gone to college, and had simplistic goals. He was also jealous of the time she spent working investigations and, in return, Gina grew tired of feeling guilty about it.

Gina gazed at the flowers and felt how lonely the last three weeks had been without Derick. They had not spoken since then, although she had wanted to call him numerous times. She didn't know what had changed to make him reconsider. Her wonderment was disturbed by Bob's firm voice asking, "So are you going to read the card or just stare at them all day?"

She smiled uneasily and pulled the card from the envelope. It read, "My baby did it again. How about dinner?" Gina's eyes sparkled and her heart raced. Derick still thought of her as "his baby."

Gina immediately sat down and dialed his number at the construction site. One of his co-workers answered and after asking for Derick, she heard echoes of men yelling, "Richards, phone." It was his voice at last.

"Richards here."

"Hello, Derick. Thanks for the beautiful flowers."

"I'm glad you like them. Gina, we need to talk and now that it looks like your part in the Timbers case is settling down, I'd like to see you tonight if that's okay."

Smiling, she replied, "I'd like to see you too. Tonight would be perfect. Can you pick me up around 7:00?"

"Sure, I'll be there."

It was already nearly 5:00 and she hurried through some paperwork that the Chief wanted completed before she left. Finally, it was done and she left the station. Her thoughts wandered on the drive home. She didn't know what Derick really wanted and she was uncertain of her own feelings. Maybe tonight would clarify it for them both.

Arriving at her apartment complex, Oak Meadows, at about 6:15 PM, she parked in space #307, jumped out of the car, and hurried to the elevator. As the doors opened, she was greeted by her neighbor, Ted, who lived across the hall.

"Hi, Gina. Why don't you make tonight the night that you finally accept my offer for dinner?"

Gina politely said, "I already have plans, but thanks anyway."

Ted seemed like a nice man, but she just wasn't interested in him. They visited in passing in the hallways, but had never gone out, despite his efforts. Ted got out of the elevator as she got in. When the doors opened for the third floor, she dashed to her apartment.

She decided she had time for a hot bath and began to fill the tub. She checked her answering machine and found a message from her best friend, Christine. Christine had heard what had happened in court and wanted to congratulate her. She had been checking on her regularly in the past few weeks since the breakup. They confided in each other openly and had been close since junior high. Gina wanted to call her back to tell her about Derick, but didn't have the time.

Gina removed her department issued weapon, a 9-millimeter SIG Sauer, from its shoulder holster and placed it in the dresser drawer beside her bed. She headed for the closet to decide what to wear. Derick didn't say where they were going, so she didn't know how to dress. But then she smiled within herself, as she remembered that Derick's idea of a nice meal was one that wasn't eaten in the truck or standing up at the construction site. Even jeans and a t-shirt would be fine with him. That was one of the things she liked about him. There was no superficiality.

While lost in thought in the closet, she heard a clicking noise from the living room balcony. She ran to the dresser drawer, got her gun, and proceeded cautiously into the living room. She knew it was probably just the wind against the door. With her gun raised, she pulled the curtains back, but saw nothing on the balcony. The sliding glass door was locked and she pulled the curtains back across the door.

She shrugged her shoulders, brought her gun down, and started to walk to her bedroom. As she started down the hallway, her thoughts again returned to Derick. Then, without warning, someone grabbed her from behind! One of his hands covered her mouth and the other knocked the gun out of her hand with a powerful blow. She whirled to confront her attacker, but couldn't get a clear picture of him. The hallway was dark. The man wore dark clothes and a black ski mask. She tried to scream, but could barely get air as he put more pressure on her mouth. He raised his other hand in front of her face and taunted her with a serrated hunting knife. He then slowly removed his hand from her mouth and turned her toward him.

While trembling fearfully, she shouted, "What do you want from me? Why are you here?"

He whispered in her ear, "You will know that I am in control. You have no power and will learn the hard way." She squirmed and kicked violently at his shins, knocking them both to the floor. They wrestled briefly before he regained control and straddled her.

Gina cried, "You won't get away with this! End it now and walk away!" With that, he hit her in the face. Blood spewed from her mouth and nose. He pulled masking tape from his coat pocket, ripped a piece off, and slapped it over her mouth. She eyed her gun lying on the floor about ten feet away, but couldn't move. He was a strong man with determination in his voice. As she struggled, he raised the knife to her throat and stopped. It was as if he couldn't decide what he wanted to do next, rape or kill her.

At that moment, there was a knock at her door. The man appeared confused.

"You make any noise and you die!"

Another knock, this time louder. Nothing. Then Derick's familiar voice bellowed, "Gina, is everything okay? Let me in and let's talk about it."

No answer. Gina prayed that Derick wouldn't leave.

Derick pleaded, "Gina, I love you. I need you in my life. I now realize no man could love you more than I do. That's enough to make it work as long as you're willing to work it out."

She had waited for what had seemed like forever for Derick to let out his true feelings. She had never imagined she would be hearing it with another man hovering over her.

Derick yelled, "I'll stand here as long as it takes! I'm not leaving!"

With that, the man jumped up and ran to the balcony. She heard him climbing down the fire escape.

Gina remained lying on the floor for a few seconds before ripping the tape from her mouth. She then ran to unlock the door. Derick's eyes dilated and his jaw dropped at the sight of her. Her shirt had patches of blood from the blow to her face and her nose continued to bleed. Without a word, Derick put his arms around her and held her tightly. Even though she was safe now, she could not stop trembling and her body whimpered from deep within her soul.

With his arm around her waist, he helped her inside and they sat down on the couch. Derick glanced around the room and heard the water running. The tub was nearly overflowing. He shut off the water and returned to the living room.

He asked, "Who did this to you?"

Gina couldn't answer. She continued to gaze out to the balcony, prompting Derick to walk towards the sliding glass door.

"Don't touch anything!" Gina cried. "There may be fingerprints."

Derick returned to the couch and continued to grill her for answers. She was afraid of what he might do and wondered what to tell him.

He asked, "Are you dating someone else? Did that man do this to you?"

That was enough. She had to tell him the truth. She went on to tell him what had happened, which really angered Derick. She had seen him lose his temper, especially when his co-worker, Stan, had made advances towards her. It had happened a couple of times before she told Derick about it. She had known how he would react, so she had tried to handle it on her own. When it appeared that she couldn't, she told Derick. He had confronted Stan at the work site and started a fight with him. The other men had had to break it up and Derick was suspended for two days.

When she finished telling him what had just happened, he asked if she had any idea who the man was. Gina said she didn't.

She picked up the phone and called her partner, Bob. Soon, there were several police officers in her apartment. Bob entered behind them with a worried look on his face.

"What can I do to help?" he asked sincerely.

Gina laughed inwardly at the irony of it all. She could not count how many times she had said the same thing to other victims.

"Help me catch this pervert!" she pleaded.

Officers were dusting for fingerprints, but she told them it was probably useless, as he was wearing gloves. She again relayed the details to Bob. She estimated the man to be about 6'0"-6'2", 200 pounds, and Caucasian. The only way she knew his race was from the openings of the ski mask. She hadn't noticed anything peculiar about his voice, as he had only whispered. Bob wanted her to go to the hospital to get checked out, but Gina didn't feel it was necessary. Paramedics who had come to the scene had stopped the bleeding from her nose and mouth. She didn't need any stitches.

She gave her full statement to Bob and they pondered over who might have done this. The fact was, in Gina's job, numerous people would have been not only capable of it, but would enjoy it as well. A series of rapes in the city over the last 8 months remained unsolved. Their only suspect had gotten off on a technicality. Gina was also reminded that Dwayne Timbers had threatened her numerous times. Yes, Timbers was in jail, but he had made it very clear that he had friends on the outside who would help him get even.

They all decided it was best to get some rest. For the time being, Bob assigned an officer to stand guard outside her apartment. Bob reluctantly handed Gina a business card. It was the number to the Rape Crisis Center, the same card they routinely gave out to women who had been assaulted.

"I don't need that!" she told him. "I wasn't assaulted!"

Bob didn't bother to argue with her about the lunacy of her statement. Gina was a very strong willed woman who would only do what she chose to do. He dropped the card on the table and left her alone in the apartment with Derick.

Derick locked the door behind him and went to the kitchen to get an ice pack from the freezer. Gina's mouth was beginning to swell, not that she had noticed. She was deep in thought. Derick handed her the ice pack and kissed her gently on the forehead. She had calmed down and appeared very tired. He sat down beside her on the couch and she rested her head against his chest.

She peered up at him and said, "This isn't quite how I imagined this evening would turn out." They laughed and held each other closely. There was no need for further words.

A knock at the door interrupted their silence. The officer at the door yelled, "There's a man by the name of Ted here who wants to see you."

Derick jumped to his feet.

"It's okay," she said, as she brushed her way past him. She checked the peephole to find the officer standing beside a worried looking Ted.

"This man says he's your neighbor and the identification checks out," informed the officer.

Gina opened the door and Ted came into the apartment. A curious Derick looked on as Ted anxiously said, "I got home a little while ago and saw the officer standing in the hallway. He told me what happened. Are you hurt?"

Derick said, "She's fine, man."

In all of the commotion, Gina had forgotten to introduce them. "Derick, this is my neighbor, Ted. Ted, this is Derick."

Ted stared at Derick, his brain simmering with curiosity.

"I'm okay, Ted. I'm just a little shaken."

Ted answered, "That's a big relief. I only wish I had been here at the time. You know you can count on me for anything, even if it's just to talk."

Derick stared intently at Ted, but did not utter a word. Gina did not like jealousy and now was not the time for it.

"I appreciate your concern, Ted. Thanks for stopping by," said Gina. Ted turned and walked out the door.

Gina smiled at the officer. "Can I get you a soda and a sandwich?" He graciously accepted and returned to his post. She made the sandwich and put it on a plate with chips, grabbed a soda from the refrigerator, and unlocked her door. As she handed him the plate and soda, he again thanked her.

Gina bolted the door and headed for the bedroom to change out of her bloodstained shirt. As she began unbuttoning it, she was startled by Derick's hand on her shoulder. She jumped uncontrollably and turned to see Derick with an uncharacteristic look of helplessness.

"I'm sorry, Derick, but I want to be alone. I'm very tired and just need to get some sleep."

"I understand," he said. "You must be exhausted from all of this, but I want to stay here with you. I'll sleep on the couch."

"Derick, that's sweet of you, but I'll be fine."

"What if the guy comes back?" he exclaimed. As soon as he said it, he wished he hadn't. "I'm sorry, Gina. I don't want to worry you any more than you already are."

She knew that was not possible. She had worked many cases like this. It was not uncommon for the intruder to return to finish the job. The man's specific intent remained a mystery to her.

After a moment's thought, she said, "I have my weapon. Besides, I have an officer at the front door." Derick finally gave up his efforts and walked dejectedly to the door. He knew her mind was made up and any further attempts would be a waste of time.

Gina followed him to the door and he gave her a caring hug. He said, "I'll call you tomorrow." She smiled and opened the door. She watched him walk down the hallway, then said goodnight to the officer, and bolted her apartment door. She double-checked the lock on the sliding glass door to the balcony, shut off the lights, and retired to her bedroom. She undressed and took a long, hot bath, which seemed to calm her nerves, and diminish the image, the ugliness. She climbed into bed with her 9-millimeter tightly clutched in her hand. He would not hurt her again.

He shoved the ski mask into a bureau drawer, disgusted with himself for the way he had handled the situation.

"You won't be so fortunate the next time, my dear Gina," he said softly.

His heart pounded in his chest at the very thought of her. She was truly frightened and he found that exhilarating. She would one day be his. On that day, his power would radiate beyond his own glory.

CHAPTER 2

Gina awoke the next morning to the sound of a ringing phone. She reached for the phone beside the bed and answered groggily, "Hello."

The comforting voice of her friend, Christine, replied in a worried tone. "Is everything okay? You didn't return my call last night."

Gina paused, not quite knowing how to tell her about it.

Christine interrupted her thoughts and burst out. "Something is wrong. I know it! I'll be right over."

Before Gina could get a word in, the line was dead. She hung up the phone and rolled over in the hopes of continuing her slumber.

Before she knew it, she was once again awakened, this time by a knocking at the door. She put a robe on, walked unsteadily to the door, and looked through the peephole. There had been a shift change, leaving a new officer standing beside Christine.

"She says she's a friend of yours?" he asked.

Gina opened the door to an excited Christine, who had a tendency to be a bit dramatic.

"What's going on? What happened to your lip?" Christine shouted.

Gina walked slowly to the couch and sat down. Christine followed and sat down beside her. Christine stared inquisitively into her eyes and placed her hand on Gina's. Christine was a very sympathetic woman. She had to be, working in social services. Gina, on the other hand, had grown colder after years of working on the street as a police officer. They had had numerous debates in terms of the punishment versus rehabilitation controversy. But they shared a strong bond of friendship and were able to put their professional differences aside.

"There was a break-in here last night," said Gina calmly.

"A break-in, what do you mean specifically?" Christine asked.

"A man broke in through the balcony," Gina answered. "He hit me and left abruptly when Derick came to the door." Christine pushed on in astonishment.

"What man hit you? Why was Derick here? Are you alright?"

Gina looked away while saying, "I'll be fine."

Christine hugged her closely, encouraging her to talk. "You need to get it all out if you're going to overcome it. You keep things bottled up and it never does you any good. I'm here to help you as a friend, Gina! Drop that cop mentality and tell me what you're feeling!"

A tear began to trickle down Gina's face and Christine gently wiped it away. Gina related the events of last night.

"Were you able to get a good look at the man?" Christine asked.

"No, it was dark. I don't know if this was a random attack or if it was related to some case I've worked. I plan to go down to the station today to review some old files."

Christine asked, "How is your lip? Does it hurt?"

"It's a little sore," Gina responded, "but it's nothing worse than the ones I got going through the Academy." They laughed and smiled as only true friends do.

"What can I do to help?" asked Christine.

"Nothing more than you've already done."

"So what happened with Derick?"

She thought for a moment. "He came to my rescue and held me closely. I went to the bedroom to change and was surprised by him. He had come into the room and touched my shoulder, which made me come unglued. He drew back and I asked him to leave. I had been so looking forward to seeing him and then I did that!"

"That was just a reflex to what had just happened, Gina. A man had you pinned down, threatening you with a knife. Of course you would be a bit jumpy from another man's touch."

"I guess so," Gina agreed.

"Well, I have to get to work," stated Christine. "Call me at work if you need anything. I'll check on you tonight."

"Thanks for everything," Gina said as they exchanged a hug good-bye.

Gina quickly got dressed and ready to go to the station. As she opened the door to the hallway, she was welcomed by the officer on duty.

"Good morning, ma'am," he piped.

"Good morning to you, too," she answered. "I don't think it's necessary to continue this watch. I'll be fine."

"I have orders to follow you, wherever you go," he replied emphatically.

Gina laughed. "I understand orders. I'm just headed to the station, anyway. You can follow me there and we can discuss it with Chief Buchanon. Okay?"

"Fine," he replied. They walked together to their cars and drove downtown to the station.

The station was all a-buzz as word of the attack on Gina had permeated conversations since last night. She knocked on the Chief's door and Buchanon yelled, "Come in!" She and the young officer serving as her protector walked in.

Chief Buchanon asked, "How are you feeling, Perry? You didn't have to come in today."

"I need to be busy," Gina replied. "I want to review some files to see if there is any link between any reported assaults and mine."

Buchanon nodded his head in agreement and she said, "There's no need for an officer guarding me. Please release this officer from his orders."

"If that's what she wants, you're free to go out on patrol, Officer Kimble," Buchanon instructed. With that, she and Officer Kimble left his office.

Gina began reviewing all of her cases from the last year involving assaults against women. Her efforts quickly narrowed in on one case. The case which had caused her the greatest grief and had threatened to ruin her career.

It involved a man by the name of John Utik. Utik was a repulsive man who had an extensive rap sheet, not only for rape, but every other crime imaginable as well. He was the classic career criminal. He had been the prime suspect in several cases she had worked over the last four years. The problem was always the same. Utik threatened and harassed the victim until they decided not to report it or press charges. Or in some cases, witnesses and victims would suddenly change their stories or claim they could not remember details.

This led to great frustrations within the police department and District Attorney's Office, as well as the community itself. Last summer, Gina and Bob thought justice would finally be served. A waitress, Shirley Jenson, was brutally raped, beaten, and left for dead in the parking lot of her apartment complex. She had apparently been followed home from the restaurant. Amazingly, she survived and was determined to testify at trial. Jenson had picked Utik out of a lineup and his fingerprints were found at the scene on her car. DNA testing also concluded with 99.89% accuracy that semen found during Jenson's medical examination was that of John Utik.

The case went to trial, as Utik claimed innocence. Jenson had been placed in protective custody after numerous threats by Utik and his friends. A department snitch had even told Gina that Utik had hired someone to kill Jenson. Jenson remained adamant that she testify. Her day came and she told the jury of the horrifying things done to her by John Utik. Gina's admiration of this woman only deepened as the trial went on. It seemed only a matter of time before the jury would render a guilty verdict. But that was not to happen.

Utik's attorney, Karen Rochester, argued that the chain of custody of evidence had been compromised. The first two officers who arrived at the scene were both rookies, just 3 weeks out of the Academy. They should never have been out on patrol together, but each of their training officers had called in sick. The dispatcher made contact with two veteran officers and told them to report to the station immediately. Before they could get to the station, the department was flooded with calls and no one was available to ride with their younger counterparts.

The lieutenant gave them some menial paperwork to do just to keep them busy. Upon completion of that, he told the two rookies to go out and get a bite to eat. By the time they got back, someone would be available. The two officers then found themselves at the wrong place at the wrong time. As they were eating a late dinner at a cafe, a woman rushed in yelling, "Someone is being attacked down the street!" The eager officers ran out in the direction the woman pointed and a block later, found a woman, later to be identified as Shirley Jenson, lying unconscious in a pool of blood.

Rochester argued vehemently that the inexperience of the officers led to contamination of the crime scene and disruption of the chain of custody. She claimed that the evidence was not properly tagged and sealed by the rookie officers and therefore, could have been tampered with or misrepresented at the lab. Rochester confused the two officers on the stand and in a surprising fashion, Judge Slocum declared that the evidence was tainted and therefore inadmissible. All that was left was Shirley Jenson's testimony. One would have thought that would have been enough by itself, but Rochester created some doubt by alleging that the police department had a vendetta against her client because they had been unable to prove him guilty of other crimes. Rochester further asserted the victim had been coaxed into picking Utik out of the lineup.

The jury's "not guilty" verdict left everyone in the courtroom astonished. It was Gina who was left with the task of comforting Shirley Jenson and telling her she had done the right thing, despite the result. Bob didn't like doing it and frequently left this part of policework to Gina. It was a difficult task with any victim, but somehow it was tenfold with Jenson. The disappointment and fear was clear on Jenson's face. Gina felt it deeply and felt partially responsible for it. After all, Gina had helped convince her to testify.

Gina took it upon herself to right the wrong on behalf of Shirley Jenson. Not only was she concerned for Jenson's safety, but Gina also felt John Utik would soon commit another crime. And when he did, Gina would be there to catch him. She followed Utik closely for weeks, even off duty. She had persuaded Bob to be involved, but Bob didn't know she was following Utik on her own at night. Utik noticed he was being tailed and contacted his attorney, Karen Rochester. Rochester filed harassment charges against the police department. Chief Buchanon was furious with both Gina and Bob. They were ordered to stay away from Utik at once. Bob did; Gina didn't.

Unbeknownst to Gina, Chief Buchanon had assigned a new undercover officer to watch her. He wanted to be certain she stayed away from Utik. It wasn't long before she was caught staking out Utik's apartment. Chief Buchanon was outraged, but afforded her one more chance. If she didn't let it go, she would be placed on suspension. Buchanon told her she was one of the best detectives he had, but she had to learn to let some cases go and not take them so personally.

That was the last day she saw Utik. He was once again the suspect in several other cases, but Chief Buchanon never assigned those cases to Gina. It may have given some the appearance of a conflict of interest, given Gina's history with Utik, and the Chief didn't want to take the risk of any further problems. The department was very fortunate that Rochester decided to drop the charges. Rochester did not state why and everyone found this curious, but were nonetheless grateful.

Gina continued to peruse past cases, particularly those involving a serrated hunting knife. She had a strong suspicion Utik was involved in the attack against her last night. He had expressed animosity towards her countless times and his physical description fit the man in her apartment. In addition, Utik had used a serrated hunting knife in his attack on Shirley Jenson.

Her continuing thoughts of the Jenson case were disturbed by a file with the name of Adams. Two months after the Jenson rape, a female firefighter by the name of Laura Adams, was raped in her apartment. A serrated hunting knife was used in the attack. Neighbors heard a struggle and called the police. When they arrived, the attacker was gone. Adams said she had been raped by a man who broke into her apartment and threatened her with some type of hunting knife that had jagged edges.

Adams was taken to the hospital for an examination, but by the time Gina arrived, Adams had decided not to file any charges and would not report any further details. Adams was a rookie firefighter and was having enough trouble with her male co-workers, who felt she was not tough enough to handle the job. As Adams had told Gina, "I don't want to add fuel to the fire."

They had both laughed at the irony of her statement and Gina partially understood how Adams felt. They never came up with any suspects on the case and it remained unsolved.

As Gina stared at the wall in deep contemplation, she heard Bob's voice as he approached her desk. He had just returned from the courthouse, where he had testified at the Dwayne Timbers trial.

"Gina, we need to talk," Bob said seriously.

"I know, Bob," she replied. "I've been reviewing some old files and think there could be a connection between Utik and all of this." Before she could continue, Bob interrupted.

"I don't think so. I think Timbers had one of his boys attack you. When I left the courthouse, I found this note on my car."

He handed her a typewritten note, which Bob had encased in a clear evidence bag. The note read: "You tell your partner to watch her back. Police work is no place for a lady. Things can get ugly."

Gina leaned back in her chair and turned to Bob. He then picked up the note and headed for the Chief's office. She followed closely behind. They showed it to Chief Buchanon, wrote up an evidence sheet, and drove to the lab.

The lab technicians found no fingerprints on the note and could not determine what type of printer was used. On the drive back to the station, Gina and Bob turned their attention to the Timbers case.

"So how did it go today?" Gina inquired.

"No problems. Timbers will be found guilty," Bob answered stoically. Then a half smile developed on his face as he said, "But then you never know how a jury will decide."

He added, "Judge Slocum recessed the case for the weekend and it will reconvene Monday morning. By the way, do you have plans for tonight? You shouldn't be alone with everything going on."

"I don't know yet," she replied.

"If you don't, come on over and have dinner with me and Lisa."

Lisa was a very nice woman who always treated Gina well. At first, Lisa was a little uneasy about her husband being partnered with a woman, but after she got to know Gina, her mind was set at ease.

"Thanks, I'll think about it."

"Are you planning on working some overtime tomorrow?" asked Bob.

"I have a lot of leads I want to check out," Gina went on fervently. "I want to talk with Shirley Jenson again to see if there is a connection between the two attacks. Maybe Utik said something similar to her. And I'm also going to try to talk with Laura Adams."Bob finally cut her off. "Slow down a minute. You don't know it was Utik who attacked you. You got yourself in enough trouble with him last time. And who is Laura Adams?"

Gina ignored the reference to Utik and continued, "Laura Adams was the firefighter who was raped in her apartment last fall. Remember, just before the attack, she was in the paper for pulling a child from a burning building?"

"Oh yeah, I remember her," Bob retorted. "She wouldn't file charges. What makes you think she'll talk to you now?"

"I don't know, I just have to try, Bob."

"What about Timbers and his friends?" Bob questioned. "What makes you think it's not them?"

Gina sighed and said, "I don't know who the hell attacked me. Maybe I just have a personal vendetta against John Utik, like the attorney, Karen Rochester claimed. Timbers has so many degenerate friends I wouldn't even know where to begin. The timing of that note could have been merely coincidental. We still don't know with certainty that I was specifically targeted."

Bob's frustration showed on his face as he implored, "Well, at least let me go with you tomorrow to talk to Jenson and Adams."

Gina replied firmly, "I appreciate your concern. But, you know they would be more comfortable talking about their attacks without the presence of a man. I'll call you if I find out anything." Bob desperately wanted to help, but knew what Gina said was true.

They pulled up to the police station, parked, and got out of the car. As they walked into the building, they exchanged "hello's" to officers. Gina returned to her desk to find a phone message from Derick. She contemplated whether she wanted to see him tonight. Her mind was so preoccupied about the attack; she didn't want to have a serious discussion with Derick about their relationship.

On the other hand, if she didn't make plans with him, Bob would expect her to come over for dinner. It wasn't that she didn't like going over to Bob and Lisa's; she just didn't want to repeat to Lisa what had happened last night. She didn't want people to pity her; she had had enough of that. She was a very independent woman who felt she could survive anything. And in some ways, she had. Her parents and siblings were killed in a car accident when she was sixteen. She was at a high school football game with Christine when it happened. Christine's family took her in until she graduated high school and got a place of her own. She had no family.

She decided to return Derick's call, but the man who answered at the construction site said he had already left for the day. She tried to reach him at home, but he wasn't there, either. She then began going through her files to locate the addresses of Shirley Jenson and Laura Adams. Paul Logan, another detective, came to her desk and said protectively, "There's a man at the front desk asking for you. His name is Derick Richards. Do you know him?"

She smiled and answered quickly, "Yes, I know him. It's okay. Thanks, Logan."

"Oh, I'm sorry," he replied in an embarrassed tone. "I guess we're all a little jumpy these days."

Gina walked up to the front desk to find Derick waiting patiently, looking around the station. He had only been there a couple times and didn't like to bother her at work.

"Hello, Gina. How are you doing?"

"Just fine."

"How about that dinner and maybe a movie?"

"Sounds good," she answered eagerly. "I'm starved; I worked through lunch. Just let me get my purse and I'll be ready."

Gina returned to her desk and told Bob she was going out with Derick. She grabbed her purse and met him in the lobby. He held the door open for her and she walked past him. "I need to take my car home first. Just follow me," she said. Derick nodded in agreement and they walked to their cars.

Across the street, a man clenched his fists in rage. *Damn! She's not alone.* He watched Derick follow her down the street. He would have to wait for a better opportunity. But it would be difficult to wait. Since last night, his intensity had built to a nearly uncontrollable level. His every thought had been of her. His insatiable hunger would have to be nourished. And soon.

Gina pulled into Oak Meadows with Derick right behind her. She got out of her car and walked over to his bright red Chevy pickup.

"I want to run upstairs and change," she told him.

Derick got out of his truck and said, "I'll come with you."

Inwardly, she was a little apprehensive about going into her apartment and was thankful Derick was with her. But she didn't want him to know or he would never leave her alone. They entered the apartment to find everything as she had left it. No notes, nothing. Derick sat down on the couch and turned on the television while Gina went into the bedroom to change.

Derick was dressed in jeans and a nice shirt, so she decided to dress casually, too. She felt uneasy about taking her gun and shoulder holster off. She decided to change into jeans, a button shirt, and dress jacket. That way, she could wear the gun in her shoulder holster undetected.

The phone rang and she hurried to it. It was Christine. "How are you doing, Gina? Do you have plans tonight?"

"I'm doing okay, really. You don't need to worry about me. Derick is here and we're getting ready to go to dinner."

Christine sounded thrilled. "Are you and Derick getting back together?"

"I don't know," Gina responded in an uneasy tone. "There are too many other things going on for me to think about it."

"I hope it all works out with the two of you," Christine commented. "I don't want to keep you, so I'll call another time. Bye."

"Good-bye," said Gina as she hung up the phone.

She returned to the living room and announced to Derick that she was ready. As they left the apartment and walked towards the elevator, she asked, "Where are we going?"

He smiled and suggested, "How about Pete's Steakhouse?"

It was his favorite restaurant and they had eaten there numerous times. Being a "meat and potato" person herself, she told him, "Sounds good to me."

They arrived at the restaurant to find a long line. They decided to wait it out and spent the time talking about how his construction job was going. The construction company he worked for, Reed and Meyers Incorporated, had won a big contract to build a hospital. He was very excited about it because it would mean steady work for awhile, in addition to bonuses and overtime.

Finally, the hostess yelled, "Richards, party of two."

With that, they were shown to their table and seated. They glanced at the menu, but ordered their regular meal of steak, baked potato, and the vegetable of the day.

Derick broke the silence. "It's so good to be spending time with you again. I've missed everything about you. Your smile, your laugh, your..."

Gina cut him off mid-sentence. "Derick, let's not put too much pressure on ourselves tonight, okay? A lot has happened and we shouldn't rush into anything."

He responded, "I understand. You can call the shots. You've been through a lot and I don't mean to pressure you." His smile was weak. Without hesitation, he asked, "Do you have any leads?"

She looked into his sympathetic eyes and said, "Nothing concrete yet, but I'm working on it." She didn't dare tell him of the threatening note left on Bob's car. There was no telling what he might do.

They enjoyed a pleasant dinner, laughing about the old times shared together. He truly was a nice man who made her feel special. They walked out of the restaurant in good spirits and climbed into his pickup.

"What movie would you like to see?" Derick asked.

She briefly looked out the window and then said, "Would you mind if we just rented a movie? I'm kind of tired and don't feel like being out in public anymore."

He grinned and said, "Sounds great. I'd rather have you all to myself, anyway."

They stopped at a video rental place and rented an action flick. Derick then suggested they stop at a liquor store and pick something up to help her unwind. She waited in the truck until he came out carrying the makings for her favorite drink, strawberry daiquiri. She thanked him for his thoughtfulness and they drove to her apartment.

Once inside, he showed her to the couch and said caringly, "You just relax. I'll make the drinks."

In no time at all, he returned with two cocktails. He set them down and sat down beside her. He leaned towards her and gave her a tender kiss. He started to hug her when he felt a solid object at her side. Gina pulled away and he opened her jacket to discover her holstered weapon. In a husky manner, he tried to jerk the weapon from its hideaway, but Gina stopped him.

His voice rising he said, "I can take care of you! You don't need this when you're with me!"

She took the gun out of her holster and stated, "This is what I do for a living. It's who I am. The fact that I carry it when I'm with you is no reflection on your masculinity. So don't pull that insecurity crap on me!"

She rose and walked to the bedroom, where she placed the gun and holster in the dresser drawer. She returned to the living room to find him guzzling his drink.

She started the movie and sat down beside him on the couch. "Thanks for the drink," she said. "It's late and we're both tired. Let's not fight about this."

He nodded his head in agreement and stared at the television. Gina knew he would sulk about it for the rest of the evening. He was overly possessive and protective of her and this had always been a big problem. She hoped it would not continue.

The movie began and the cocktails disappeared in no time. Gina had been wound pretty tight all day and seemed to be relaxing better with the help of the alcohol. She didn't drink very often and she began feeling very sleepy. She got up and refilled their drinks with the remainder in the blender. They snuggled together on the couch and fell asleep in each other's arms.

CHAPTER 3

Sunlight filtering in through the slats in the venetian blinds awakened their deep slumber and they got up slowly.

"How about going to breakfast?" Derick asked.

"No thanks, I have to leave for work," Gina responded.

"I have to work today, too, and better get going. Have a good day!"

He kissed her gently and left the apartment. Gina hurriedly took a shower and got dressed. She hoped that she would get some answers today and develop more leads.

A while later she was at Charlie's, the restaurant where Shirley Jenson continued to work as a waitress. She walked in and stood at the doorway. A moment later, Shirley walked out of the kitchen and spotted her. Shirley sighed deeply before walking towards her.

Gina smiled sympathetically and said, "I hate to put you through this again, but I need to ask you a few questions."

As Shirley's eyes began to tear up, she murmured, "Did it do any good last time? I'm doing everything I can to put it all behind me and get on with my life!"

"I just need a few minutes," Gina pressed. "There's been another attack and it could be the same man."

Shirley desperately glanced around the restaurant as if she was looking for a customer to wait on to avoid talking to Gina. But the lunch crowd had not arrived and the place was empty. Shirley hesitantly said, "Okay, but just for a minute! If my boss comes out, you have to go." Gina nodded in agreement and they sat down at the booth near the door.

Gina eagerly began, "During the attack, did Utik say anything to you? I looked at your statement, but it didn't address this."

Shirley shrugged her shoulders and said, "I remember you asking me that question after it happened, but I couldn't remember anything. He kept hitting me until I blacked out."

"Do you remember anything else about the knife you didn't tell us before?"

"No," Shirley said firmly. The kitchen door swung open and an overweight, bald man walked to the counter.

"I gotta go," said Shirley as she hurried back to the kitchen.

Gina left the restaurant and headed for her car. She unlocked the car, got in, and searched her notes for Laura Adams' home address. She hoped it would prove to be more fruitful.

As she pulled up to Laura Adams' apartment complex, she spotted her in the lot, washing her car. It certainly was a beautiful day for it. The sun was out, yet it wasn't too hot. Spring had arrived a little early this year.

Gina parked her car in the visitor section and proceeded to walk towards Adams. As she neared, Adams looked up and saw her. Gina held out her badge while saying, "Ms. Adams, my name is Gina Perry. I'm a detective with the police department. You may not remember me, but I spoke with you briefly at the hospital after you were attacked."

Laura Adams picked up the bucket of water and rags she was using to wash the car and pushed past Gina. Gina followed, prompting Adams to lash out. "Leave me alone! I have nothing to say to you!"

Gina persisted, even though Adams continued to walk to the apartment. "There's been another attack. It's never going to end if you and other women remain silent!"

Adams entered the apartment and slammed the door behind her. Gina started to walk away, but decided to try a different approach.

Gina stood in front of her doorway and pleaded, "I told you that another woman was attacked. That woman was me!"

With that, the door opened and Adams showed Gina in. Gina sat down on the living room couch and Adams sat in the recliner. It was a small apartment with all kinds of weight lifting equipment surrounding them. Adams noticed Gina looking around and smiled.

"I know it seems a bit much, but I have to stay in good shape to be a firefighter."

Gina laughed and added, "I can relate. While I was going through the Police Academy, I lifted more weights than I care to remember."

Gina began the real conversation with empathy. "I'm sorry I have to bother you about this, but I must if I'm ever going to catch the guy, Ms. Adams."

"Please call me Laura. Ms. Adams makes me feel old and I'm only 25." They both smiled at one another as thoughts raced through Gina's mind. She didn't know how open this woman would be and didn't want to overwhelm her all at once.

Gina asked, "Have you told anyone what happened to you that night?"

Laura looked away as she answered, "No."

"How have you been handling it on your own?"

"I've managed to get by," Laura said. "I don't want to be afraid anymore."

"Neither do I! That's why I need your help to put this guy away," said Gina.

Laura still seemed reluctant to discuss the matter, so Gina tried to carry the conversation. "A man broke into my apartment two nights ago and threatened me with a knife. He was either planning to rape or kill me, maybe even both. He was interrupted by someone at my door and he fled my apartment."

"So you weren't raped?" Laura exclaimed.

"No, not yet. I received a threatening note the next morning."

"What do you want from me?" Laura implored.

Gina leaned towards her and calmly stated, "I need you to tell me what happened to you that night. I want to compare notes to determine if the same man attacked both of us and possibly other women. He must be stopped before he victimizes someone else. Would you want another woman to have to go through what you've been through?"

"Of course not! What do you think I am?" Laura exclaimed.

Gina responded softly, "I think you're a woman who is going through a lot of internal pain and until you admit it, things won't improve. I'm the last person to talk about this because I'm very similar to you. I always think I can handle it on my own. We work in jobs that are dominated by men and often have to be self-sufficient, and this carries over into our personal lives. It's difficult to separate the two. But in order for you to have closure, you need to do something constructive about this, like helping me catch this weirdo."

Laura sat pensively in silence for a moment before saying, "I don't even know where to begin. It was all so horrible."

"Just start with the events of that day," Gina said.

Laura leaned back in her chair and began, "Everything had been going so well that week. I had been at the scene of an apartment building fire and had pulled a child out of it. I immediately was swarmed by reporters wanting the full story. I had finally won the respect of my male co-workers and I was on an emotional high. Three days later, that high ended. I came home after working a long shift and immediately headed for the bedroom to get changed. I began to undress when a man grabbed me from behind. He covered my mouth and told me if I made noise, he'd kill me. I have no idea how he even got in here." Laura stopped talking and looked away, her gaze distant.

Gina moved closer to Laura and held her trembling hand. Gina asked, "What happened next?"

"I did what he said," Laura replied matter-of-factly. "Maybe I should have fought him more, but I truly believed he would kill me if I resisted. Besides, he had a big knife with jagged edges pointed at me the whole time. He threw me down on the bed, tore off my clothes, and raped me. I cried through it all, but this didn't bother him in the least. In fact, he seemed to enjoy it even more."

Gina paused for a moment before asking, "Did he say anything else to you?"

"He said that I must think I was a big hero now and that he would knock me down a peg or two."

"Do you have any idea who the man was?" Gina asked.

"At first, because of the statement he made, I thought it may have been one of the guys at work. Maybe one of them was jealous that it was me who saved that little girl. I never saw the man's face because he had a dark ski mask on the entire time. But I did get a good look at the rest of him, particularly his chest, which was very hairy. I went so far as to start playing basketball at the park in the afternoons with some of the guys at work. I knew it would get hot and they would take their shirts off. Then I could see if any of them resembled the man who raped me. But none of them did."

"Have you received any threatening notes or phone calls since then?"

"No, I haven't. It seems to have all ended," Laura said thankfully.

"This man picked you for a reason and I think mine was a planned assault, too," Gina speculated. "He told me he was in control, not me, and I would learn the hard way. There was something about the way he said it which makes me believe it was not your average pervert off the street."

Gina asked, "Was there anything else peculiar about him, like an accent, an odor, or a particular way he did something?"

A silence hung heavy for what seemed like hours and then Laura spoke. "He didn't say much and when he did, he only whispered; I didn't notice anything peculiar about his speech. Nor did I detect any unusual odor. But one thing was clear; he was a control freak! At first, he told me to take off my clothes and when I didn't do it as quickly as he wanted, he violently ripped them off himself. After he was through with me, he methodically got dressed and then began wiping all of the furniture in the bedroom with a cloth he pulled out of his jacket pocket. When he first grabbed me, he was wearing gloves, but he took them off shortly after that."

"There is something else I have to ask. You were checked out at the hospital and the pelvic examination found no semen present."

"He wore a condom. He was not some low life off the street who decided at the last minute to rape me. He was well prepared and was very calculating."

"Can you describe his overall appearance?" Gina asked.

Without much delay, Laura informed, "He was white, at least 6 feet tall, and maybe 210 pounds."

"Can you tell me anything more about the knife?"

Laura paused before muttering, "It was about 5 or 6 inches long with jagged edges. The handle was a dark color. I don't remember anything else."

"How are you feeling now?" Gina asked.

"Surprisingly, better than I thought I would have been after telling you all this. But I still don't want to press charges and I'm firm about that. I hope the information I've given you is of some help. Now I have to get ready to go to work."

They shook hands and Gina handed her a business card in case she thought of anything further. Gina thanked her for her help and then walked to the car. The interview had left her more confused than ever.

On the way to the station, Gina stopped at McDonald's to pick up some lunch. At the station, she sat down at her desk and began eating her lunch. Detective Logan walked over to her and said, "Looks like it's just you and me working up here today."

"Yeah, I guess we're the lucky ones, Logan," she added.

"Have you had any breaks on your case?"

"No, but I'm working on it."

He politely offered, "Well, if you need any help, let me know."

"Thanks, I will."

As Detective Logan began to walk away, he turned around and said, "I know you're busy, but I have a lady coming in to give a statement and it would be better to have another detective in the interview, especially a woman. Detective Rogers was supposed to be in, but he called in sick. This interview won't take long."

Gina could not resist Logan's boyish charm and genuine smile.

"Sure, I'll do it. When is the woman coming in?" she asked.

"In about a half hour. Go ahead and finish your lunch. Thanks, Gina."

As she ate, she pondered over what Laura Adams had told her. There were some similarities between the attacks on Adams, Shirley

Jenson, and herself. Of course, there had been other rapes and assaults against women, but the attackers did not fit the description as closely and did not use the same type of knife as the one in question.

This attacker was of the same physical description in all three cases. He also used the same type of serrated hunting knife. But his method of operation was drastically different. He attacked Jenson in a parking lot, beat her senselessly, and didn't wear a condom during the rape. The lab tests had determined with 99.89% accuracy that the semen found during Jenson's medical examination was that of John Utik. Furthermore, the man left fingerprints at the scene and these were later identified as Utik's.

On the contrary, the man who raped Laura Adams was much smarter. He attacked Adams in her apartment, wore protection, and wiped the place clean for fingerprints. The man who broke into Gina's apartment was wearing gloves and left no prints at the scene. To both herself and Adams, he had made some comment about control or knocking them down a peg. They appeared to be chosen victims. Because Jenson had been beaten to unconsciousness, she could not recall any specific comments made by her attacker and could give only sketchy details. Adams felt she could identify this man by his hairy chest and had gone out of her way to check out her male co-workers. But how many men in the world would that description fit?

There were clues which tended to link the attacks and others which seemed to separate them. Had John Utik become more careful or was it not the same man at all? Gina's mind raced with various facts and theories until she was interrupted by the sound of approaching footsteps.

Detective Logan appeared at Gina's desk and announced, "That witness is here. She's waiting in the interview room." Gina stood up and followed Logan into the room, where they found a concerned-looking homemaker by the name of Mary Thompson.

Logan introduced everyone. "Mrs. Thompson, this is Detective Perry. Detective Perry, Mrs. Thompson."

In a nervous tone, Mrs. Thompson said, "I don't understand why I had to come in today and repeat what I told the uniformed officers last night."

Logan explained, "We just need you to make a formal statement and answer a few follow up questions, okay?"

"Very well," Mrs. Thompson agreed.

"The incident report shows that you made a 911 call at 10:28 PM last night. Is that correct?" Logan asked.

"Yes, I was watching television when I heard a noise outside. I went to the window and looked at the house next door, in the direction I had heard the noise. I saw someone hiding in the shrubs in the yard next door. I watched as he crept closer to the house. I then grabbed the portable phone and called 911 while I continued to watch him. He was hiding behind the shrubbery near the living room window. I could see the silhouette of my neighbor, Denise, through the window. He stared intently at her until the living room light went out and all was dark. He then pulled a knife out of his pocket and began to cut the window screen. As he was doing that, Denise's husband, Mark, pulled into the driveway. The man saw him coming and hid behind the bushes until Mark went into the house. The man then snuck off before the police got there."

Logan questioned her further, "What did the man look like?"

"He was wearing dark clothing and a ski mask over his face. I couldn't even tell you his race."

"Was he short or tall, heavy or thin?"

"He just seemed to be of an average build, I guess; I told the officers that last night."

"Could you estimate his height or weight?"

In a confused tone, she told them, "I don't know how to guess someone's height or weight. I just don't pay that much attention."

Gina intervened, "I understand, Mrs. Thompson. It is difficult to estimate those kinds of things. But just for the sake of comparison, I want you to take a look at Detective Logan."

Gina looked at him and said, "Will you please stand up?"

Logan complied with her request and Gina continued.

"Did the man look taller or shorter than Detective Logan?"

"Oh, he looked taller, by a couple inches."

"How would he compare to Detective Logan in terms of weight?"

Mrs. Thompson hesitantly said, "He wasn't built as well as this detective, if you know what I mean?"

She grinned at Gina and Gina smiled in return. Gina definitely knew what she meant. Logan was very brawny and she had noticed that a long time ago.

Gina asked, "You mean the man wasn't as muscular?"

Mrs. Thompson laughed and said, "Yes, that's what I mean. The man wasn't overweight, but he just looked to be of an average build."

Detective Logan sat back down in his chair and smiled at Gina. He picked up where Gina left off.

"I'm about 5'10" and 180 pounds. So this guy was about 6 feet tall and maybe 190 pounds?"

"Maybe a little heavier," she answered.

Logan proceeded, "What about the knife? Can you tell us anything about it?"

"No, the only way I could tell it was a knife was because I saw the flash of the blade from the light glaring out of the window. The police looked at the screen last night, but he had just begun cutting it, so there wasn't much damage done."

Logan asked in closing, "Do you know of anyone who would want to harm your neighbor?"

Mrs. Thompson shrugged her shoulders and commented, "It could have been anyone, given Denise's line of work. I told her that when she first took that job, but she said I was just being paranoid."

"What does she do for a living?" Logan asked.

"She's a probation officer."

Logan began to speak, but was quickly interrupted by Gina's excited words.

"You said her name was Denise. What's her last name?"

"Steidman."

Gina's heart pounded as ideas rushed through her mind. Logan thanked Mrs. Thompson for coming in and walked her to the door. Gina followed and wished her a nice day. After they parted, Gina raced to the file room with Logan at her heels.

"What's wrong?" he asked, with a perplexed look on his face.

She grabbed a folder from the file cabinet and set it down on a nearby table. The name of the file was written in boldface letters on the cover: Timbers, Dwayne. She pointed at it and exclaimed, "This is what's wrong!"

Logan answered in dismay, "What could Timbers possibly have to do with this? As you're well aware, he's currently in jail while on trial for killing his girlfriend."

Gina quizzed him, "The name of Denise Steidman doesn't ring any bells with you?"

Logan replied, "Not before today."

She explained, "A few years ago, Dwayne Timbers was placed on probation for breaking and entering. Steidman was Timber's probation officer! He completed his probation shortly before he killed his girlfriend. Although he had completed his probation requirements, Steidman had asserted he was a continuing danger to society and tried to get the probation extended. However, her efforts met with negative results. Steidman actually testified for the prosecution at his current trial. She told the jury her experiences with this man had her convinced he was a very diabolical man who could not, and would not, conform to the rules of a civilized society. She added that although he was placed on probation for breaking and entering, he had actually assaulted another girlfriend in her home, but it had been pled down to breaking and entering."

Logan stood there stunned and finally asked, "You think Dwayne Timbers hired someone on the outside to kill Steidman?"

"Anything is possible, right?" Gina replied with an odd look on her face. "I really thought it was Utik who attacked me Thursday night, but now I don't know. That note left on Bob's car at the courthouse could have also been left by a messenger of Timbers."

Logan persisted, "If that is in fact true, who do you think would have done it for Timbers?"

"He has a cousin who has done some time, as well as many friends. I'm not sure."

She picked up the folder and took it to her desk for further review. Logan followed and added, "It sounds like this could get complicated."

She smiled mysteriously and said, "I think so."

Logan walked to his desk and placed a call to Denise Steidman to set up an interview, but she wasn't home. He returned to Gina's desk and glanced over her shoulder at the various contents of the Timbers folder. After a few minutes, he broke the silence.

"I have to get going, but I'll keep trying to get in touch with Steidman over the weekend. It will be interesting to know if she has received any threats since she testified at the Timbers trial. I'll let you know what I find out."

Gina looked up and said, "Please do. Have a good weekend." He grabbed his jacket and headed downstairs.

Gina's phone rang and she answered, "Detective Perry."

"Hi Gina, it's Christine. How did I know I'd find you there on a Saturday?"

"Dumb luck, I guess. What are you up to today?"

"I've enjoyed a quiet day around the apartment. But I wanted to see if you would like to come over for dinner tonight. There's someone I want you to meet."

Gina giggled and said, "No way, Christine. I'm not letting you set me up again. That last guy made the guys at work look appealing."

Christine agreed, "You're right; that didn't work out as I had hoped. But actually, I'm not trying to set you up this time. I met this man a few weeks ago and we have been dating ever since."

Gina was astonished, "A few weeks ago? Why didn't you tell me about him?"

Christine replied rather reluctantly, "Well, you and Derick had just broken up and I didn't want to make you feel worse by telling you about this wonderful man I was seeing. Ironically, he works for the same construction company as Derick, but he says he doesn't know Derick very well."

"I'm very happy that you've found someone you enjoy spending time with, Christine. But I don't know if I would be the best company tonight."

"Come on, Gina," Christine pleaded. "I respect your opinions and am grateful to have a friend who is so candid. I want you to meet him and tell me what you think. Please?"

With much hesitation, Gina asked, "What do you want me to bring and at what time?"

Christine gleefully said, "Just come over around 6:30. He's actually doing all the cooking himself, so you don't need to bring anything. Gina, I think I could really fall for this guy." They exchanged good-byes and Gina hung up the phone. It was already nearly 5 PM, so she decided she'd better wrap things up and head for home.

When she arrived at Oak Meadows, she found a couple of broken beer bottles in her parking space. Some of the locals started drinking early, she surmised. She parked in a different space and went up to her apartment to get a pair of gloves and a bag to put the glass in. She knew from past experience that if she didn't clean it up, it would stay there for some time. As she unlocked the door, the phone began ringing. She quickly slammed the door behind her, dropped her purse on the kitchen counter, and grabbed the phone on the third ring.

"Hello," she said out of breath.

It was Derick. "Hi Gina, how was your day?"

"It was okay. How about yours?"

He said proudly, "Fine, my crew got a lot of work done today." He paused and then asked, "Would you like to go out tonight?"

"I would, but I've already made plans with Christine. How about we take a raincheck?"

"Okay, have a good time with Christine."

"You have a good evening, too. Bye, Derick."

She snatched a grocery bag from under the kitchen sink and got a pair of gloves from the hallway closet. She walked down to the parking lot to pick up the broken glass. As she bent over picking up pieces of the broken bottles, her mind wandered to John Utik and Dwayne Timbers. They were both capable of anything and had expressed a deep hatred of her. Her thoughts were interrupted by the sound of a car horn. Her body flinched as she turned to see her neighbor, Ted, pulling into the lot. He got out and walked over to her. "I'm sorry, Gina, I didn't mean to startle you."

She said in an embarrassed manner, "That's okay. I've just been a little uptight the last few days."

Ted smiled and said, "That's understandable, given what you've been through. Have you caught the guy yet?"

"No, but I will."

Ted stared at the broken bottles and asked, "Who did this?"

She shrugged her shoulders, "Probably just some of the college kids downstairs."

Ted nodded his head in agreement and began to help her pick up the scattered glass. Just as Gina was about to offer him a glove, Ted flinched. He had cut one of his fingers on his right hand on a piece of glass. Gina immediately grabbed his hand to look at the cut. Blood was streaming out of his index finger.

She announced, "Let's go upstairs and wash this out. You also need to apply some pressure to control the bleeding."

As with any other man, Ted replied, "It's not that bad. I'll be fine."

She looked deeply into his eyes and even though they didn't know each other very well, Ted could surmise that arguing with her would be a losing battle.

"Okay, I'll go."

She grabbed the bag full of glass and they headed upstairs.

"Come on in," she said, as she opened her door. He followed her to the kitchen sink and she held his hand under the water until the cut was clean. "I'm really sorry this happened."

He nonchalantly replied, "It's nothing; don't worry about it, Gina."

She wrapped a hand towel around his finger and applied pressure to it. She then told him, "Hold this while I get a bandage." He did and she left the room.

She returned a moment later and removed the towel. The cut had stopped bleeding and fortunately, wasn't that deep.

Gina efficiently bandaged the finger and glanced up at Ted, who was gazing down at her. They had never been that close to one another and she felt a bit of tension. Ted began to lean towards her and she pulled away. "It looks like it's going to be fine," she murmured.

"I'm sure of it," he said.

Ted then took the hint and walked towards the door. She found it so refreshing to be around a man who knew when it was time to leave. As he opened the door, she again thanked him for his help.

He smiled, "Anytime."

Gina locked the door behind him and quickly got ready to go to Christine's. She then raced downstairs to her car and headed across town. On the way over, she replayed the conversation with Christine over and over in her mind. She was so thrilled that Christine had found someone special. Her friend was a wonderful person who deserved the best in life, unlike Christine's last boyfriend who was involved with other women during their relationship.

Gina arrived at Christine's apartment at about 6:40 PM. She knocked on the door and was greeted by Christine, who gave her a big hug.

"I'm sorry for being a little late."

"Oh, no problem. I thought you might have changed your mind about coming."

Gina grinned and asked, "So where is he?"

Christine pulled her arm and said, "In the kitchen, come on."

Christine led her through the living room and into the kitchen, where his back was to them. Christine said enthusiastically, "Honey, Gina's here!"

He turned around and Gina leaned back against the counter in sheer amazement. Her pulse raced and she felt a familiar pit in her stomach. Christine smiled deliriously and introduced them, "Gina, this is Stan. Stan, this is my best friend, Gina."

Gina had no idea how to respond. Stan broke the silence in a cordial manner, "Oh, I didn't know it was you. Christine just told me she had a friend she wanted me to meet."

Christine looked bewildered and asked, "Do you two know each other?"

Before Gina could answer, Stan interjected, "I'd seen her around the construction site when she was visiting Richards."

Gina carefully chose her words, "Yes, it's a small world, isn't it?" she said stammering. Apparently, Stan hadn't said anything about Gina to Christine. Gina sighed in frustration, for the man whom her best friend believed was too good to be true, was in fact just that.

Stan had repeatedly made unwanted sexual advances towards Gina in the past while she was dating Derick. This was the same man whom Derick had fought with at work a couple months ago, causing Derick to be suspended without pay. Should she tell Christine the truth right away, wait until later, or let her find out on her own what kind of man she was seeing? One thing was certain. It was sure to be an interesting evening.

CHAPTER 4

Stan declared, "Dinner is almost ready. Why don't you ladies just have a seat at the table and leave the rest to me?"

As Gina and Christine sat down, Christine exclaimed, "Isn't he unbelievable?"

Gina concurred and said, "That he is."

The table was already set, complete with champagne flutes. Gina had to admit the aroma coming from the kitchen was divine.

"What is he cooking?" she asked.

Christine gleamed with delight, "Some type of seafood pasta."

Stan brought out two steaming plates of pasta and placed them in front of the women. He left the room and returned with his own serving and a bottle of Korbel Brut Extra Dry. He set down his plate and popped the cork on the champagne. He then slowly filled their flutes and said, "I propose a toast to new friendships and lasting love." They all clinked their glasses and took a drink. Stan then leaned across the table and kissed Christine. Gina looked away.

Beaming, Stan said, "Dig in, while it's still hot." They began eating and the silence returned.

"So how did the two of you meet?" Gina asked.

"It was fate," Christine answered naively. "I was at a gas station and he pulled up on the other side of the pump. I was trying to top off the gas and it overflowed all down the side of my car. He noticed I was all dressed up for work and offered to wipe it off for me." Christine smiled at Stan and took a bite from her plate.

"And then what?" Gina inquired.

"Then he asked me if I'd like to go out for a drink sometime."

"And the rest is history," Stan interjected.

Gina ate her meal in silence and wished the evening would end quickly. She wanted to tell Christine about Stan, but now was not the time. Her mind wandered to other things and she remembered she hadn't called Bob to tell him about the case. She would have to do that when she got home, if it wasn't too late.

Dinner finally ended and so did the small talk. They began clearing the table and Stan insisted he do the dishes. Gina and Christine retired to the living room and sat down on the couch. With much anticipation, Christine turned to Gina and asked, "So what do you think about Stan?" Gina didn't quite know how to answer her.

"You seem very happy."

"Oh, I am!" Christine exclaimed. "I had forgotten there were still a few nice men left in the world."

Gina smiled and tried to change the subject.

"I know what you mean. Derick can be very sweet at times, but something still doesn't feel right. And on the other hand, a chance encounter with my neighbor, Ted, left me feeling even more confused. Remember, I've told you about Ted. He's always seemed liked a nice man, yet I was never interested in him."

Christine asked, "You mean you are interested in him now?"

"I'm not sure. He just seems so gentle and easy going. He seems secure and not the type to be so jealous of everything, like Derick."

"Derick is a nice man who would do anything for you, Gina. Isn't that enough?"

"I don't know what I want anymore. However, I do know I want someone with whom I can share a meaningful conversation and intimate feelings. That's not Derick's style. He can be rather dense at times."

Stan walked into the living room and said, "I've enjoyed the evening, ladies. I think I'll head home and let you continue your girl talk."

He looked suspiciously over at Gina when she said, "Thanks for the dinner, Stan. It was delicious."

"You're welcome. Let's do it again real soon."

He turned and headed for the door with Christine following. They exchanged a long kiss at the door and then he was gone.

Christine returned to the living room with a huge grin on her face. She looked at Gina and her face grew more concerned.

"Why don't you like him?"

"What's not to like?" responded Gina.

In a disappointed tone, Christine asked, "What happened to your blatant honesty, Gina?"

"I can see that you're very happy and I don't want to spoil it for you."

"How could you spoil it for me?"

Gina said in a reserved tone, "I think he's trying too hard to make you like him, by making dinner and even doing the dishes. Even some of the things he said don't really sound like him. He's saying what he thinks you want to hear."

"What do you mean it doesn't sound like him? How would you know? Did you overhear him talking to some of the men at the construction site while you were visiting Derick?"

Gina let out a deep sigh as she said, "You want my complete honesty, right?"

Christine answered emphatically, "Of course, Gina! What is it?"

"I've been wondering how to tell you this all evening. Stan is not the man you think he is. Did he tell you anything about me?"

"No, nothing."

Gina continued, "The fact is he and I had spoken several times before tonight. Do you remember a few months ago, when I told you that a man at Derick's construction site kept making sexual advances towards me and when I told Derick about it, they got into a fight?"

"Yes, I remember, but what does that have to do with Stan?"

Gina looked deeply into Christine's eyes, "That man was Stan."

Christine's jaw dropped. "Why are you making this all up? Are you that jealous of my new relationship?"

"I understand you're upset. You have every right to be. But I'm not making anything up and you know it."

Looking sheepish now she said, "You're right. I'm sorry. Tell me more about it. I need to know."

"Maybe you should be discussing this with Stan."

Christine assertively said, "Believe me, I will. But I want to hear it from you."

Gina reluctantly agreed to continue. "It happened three or four times. He kept asking me out, even though he knew I was dating Derick. I politely told him I wasn't interested. He would say something offensive or try to touch me in some way. One time, he purposely ran into me and touched my breasts. He said it was just an accident. On the last occasion, he cornered me and started kissing me. I was struggling with him and fortunately, another construction worker walked in. Stan backed off. I then felt compelled to tell Derick about it. He got extremely angry and got into a fight with Stan at work. The other men had to pull Derick off of Stan. Derick was suspended without pay for two days."

Christine inquired, "Why didn't you say something earlier tonight?"

Gina shrugged her shoulders. "I was so shocked when I saw him here, that I didn't know quite how to react. I didn't know what he had told you about me, either. Knowing Stan, he'll deny all of this and try to break up our friendship. He was very bitter about being rejected."

Christine covered her face with her hands in obvious disappointment. Gina tried to comfort her by putting her arm around her and holding her closely. Christine began crying and asked, "Why is it I can't seem to find a decent man to love? Are there none left in this world?"

Gina's voice was soothing, "They're out there. We just haven't found them yet. But one day we will and we'll appreciate them even more."

Christine whined, "How can you be so sure? We've both had our share of heartbreaks. I was falling in love with Stan and had no idea what he was really like. Think about it, Gina. I've slept with the same man who was trying to force himself on you!"

Their conversation was interrupted by a loud knock at the door. Christine wiped the tears from her face and headed for the door. She opened it and saw a derelict holding a bouquet of spring flowers. He asked with slurred speech, "Are you Gina Perry?"

"No, but she's here."

He handed her the flowers and staggered down the hallway.

Christine walked back to the living room, but Gina was nowhere in sight. Christine yelled, "Gina!" Gina walked out of the kitchen with a soda in hand. Christine stated, "These are for you. Some drunk just delivered them."

Gina grabbed the card from the flowers. It read: "Wherever you are, I won't be far."

In a demanding fashion, Gina grabbed Christine's hand and led her quickly out of the apartment building. They ran outside and Gina asked, "Do you see the man who delivered them?" They looked in the parking lot and down the street in both directions before Christine shouted, "There he is!" Christine pointed to a bum who was digging through a dumpster in a nearby lot.

Gina ran over to the man and screamed, "Who gave you the flowers to deliver?" His body swayed from side to side as he muttered, "Who wants to know?"

Gina quickly showed him her shield and demanded, "You tell me everything you know or I'm taking you in!"

The man immediately began talking. "Some guy gave me a pint of Jack Daniels to deliver those flowers. He told me I had to drink the whiskey first."

"What did the man look like?"

"I don't remember, lady. He was just another bum off the street, like me. I'd never seen him before."

She asked, "What else did that bum tell you?"

The man belched loudly and then replied, "He said some guy gave him a pint of whiskey for him to hand over the flowers and address to someone else. He was soused, too."

"How long ago and where did this happen?"

"I don't know, just long enough for me to drink the pint on the way over here."

The man suddenly sat down on the pavement and began singing bits and pieces of some jazz song. He was unresponsive and Gina knew she would get nothing else out of him. He was so drunk that she knew she was lucky to have found out anything. It was very clear whoever sent those flowers had covered his tracks well. Not only had he gotten two bums involved, he had them drink the whiskey first. That way, it was unlikely they would remember specific details or link him to it in any way.

Christine and Gina slowly walked back to the apartment. Christine then poured a glass of champagne and asked Gina if she would like one.

"No thanks," Gina answered. She sat in silence, coldly staring at the flowers and card.

"What's going on?" Christine asked in confusion.

"Since my attack on Thursday night, I believe someone has been stalking me. A threatening note, directed at me, was left on Bob's car and now this. Christine, nobody even knew I was having dinner with you. Someone must have followed me here."

Christine appeared rather shocked. Finally, she asked Gina, "Is it the same man who attacked you?"

"I think so. But I still don't know who it is. I'd better call Bob and let him know what's going on. I was in a hurry when I got here and left my cell phone in the car. May I use your phone?"

"Sure."

Gina went to another room to use the phone and Christine continued to sip on her champagne in the living room. After a short time, Gina returned to the living room and sat down.

"Bob's on his way over. He wants to follow me home and see if he spots anyone. I'm going to leave in about fifteen minutes. He will be parked across the street at the gas station. When I leave, he'll follow. Bob is hoping the mystery man is waiting for me outside and we can put an end to all of this tonight."

"I hope it all works out!" Christine exclaimed.

After fifteen minutes of seemingly endless waiting, Gina left Christine's apartment. As she left the building, she glanced around the parking lot. She didn't notice anything out of the ordinary. Her heart pounded as she quickly made her way to her car. She looked inside and around the car, but saw nothing. She unlocked the door and got in.

She drove out of the lot and spotted Bob waiting across the street. She casually glanced in the rear view mirror, but didn't detect anyone following her. After she had driven about a block away, Bob pulled out onto the street behind her. It was an uneventful drive home. Gina pulled into Oak Meadows and parked in space 307. As soon as she turned the ignition off, her cell phone rang.

Gina answered, "No luck, huh?"

She was surprised to hear Derick's voice say, "What are you talking about, Gina? Where have you been?" His voice was mumbled and shaky. There was music and loud voices in the background; he was apparently at a bar.

She replied, "I told you. I had plans with Christine. I just pulled up to my apartment. Have you been drinking?"

"What's it to you, anyway?" Derick intoned.

Gina remained seated in her car, deeply involved in the conversation. After a moment's silence, Derick announced, "I'm coming over right now, whether you like it or not."

Gina insisted, "No, you're not. You go home and sleep it off and we'll talk when you're sober. I don't want to see you like this!" The line went dead and Gina started to get out of the car.

As she arose, she was stunned by the sight of a figure walking towards her. The parking lot lighting was dim and she could not make out a face. As she reached for her gun, another figure ran up behind the first figure and jumped on him. The two bodies wrestled on the ground and Gina ran over to them. She recognized Bob's voice as he yelled, "I've got him, Gina!"

Gina was astonished by what she saw. There was Bob, straddling the supposed rapist, with his gun pointed at the man's head. And beneath Bob, lay an overpowered, frightened looking Ted.

Gina yelled at Bob, "It's not him! Back off!"

A confused looking Bob said, "I watched this guy follow you into the lot and approach your vehicle!"

"This is my neighbor, Ted. I know him."

Bob got up and helped Ted to his feet. Gina placed her hand on Ted's shoulder and said, "I'm so sorry. Are you alright?"

A shaken Ted replied, "Yes, I'm okay." Ted glanced in wonder at Bob, not knowing why he was there.

Gina introduced them, "Ted, this is my partner, Bob. Bob, this is Ted, who lives across the hall from me."

With much chagrin, Ted admitted, "I saw you sitting in your car when I pulled into the lot. I just wanted to come over to talk to you. I didn't mean to scare you. I guess I should have known better than to walk up to you like that at night, with everything you've been through. I'm sorry, Gina."

She answered in a soft-spoken voice, "It's okay."

Bob extended his hand to Ted and said, "No hard feelings?"

"None at all," Ted replied.

With that, they all turned and began walking towards the apartment building. Gina ran back to her car to get her purse and the flowers. All three went into the building and rode the elevator up to the third floor. Bob followed Gina into her apartment and they said goodnight to Ted, who was unlocking his door across the hall.

Bob walked to the phone and told Gina, "I'm assigning an officer to stand guard in the hallway. Don't try to talk me out of it." He called the station and was told that an officer would be on the way.

"Can I get you anything to drink?" Gina asked.

"No thanks."

Gina showed Bob the flowers and card she had received. She had wrapped the card in a clear sandwich bag at Christine's, in the hopes that it may have prints on it. She asked him, "What do you make of all this?"

Bob hesitated before responding, "I think somebody out there really wants to make a point to you. He's not going to simply disappear, Gina."

After a moment's reflection, she asked, "Then how do we make him reappear quickly?"

"We don't. He'll make a move soon enough. Now you'll have 24-hour protection and when he comes around, they will stop him before he ever gets to you. In the meantime, we'll follow up on more leads and maybe we can determine who this guy is before he ever tries anything else. By the way, how well do you know your neighbor, Ted?"

Gina answered calmly, "Not that well. Why?"

"No reason, I was just curious. What are your plans for tomorrow?"

"I'm not sure, yet," she replied.

"I'll take the card and flowers to the lab. Maybe we'll get lucky and lift some prints."

They heard a knock at the door and Bob said, "I'll get it. It's probably the cop who's going to stand guard." Bob walked to the door and looked through the peephole. He announced, "It's Derick, Gina. Are you two getting back together?"

She answered nervously, "I don't know, but I don't want to talk to him right now. He called me on my cell phone right when I pulled up; that's why I was distracted. He was obviously drunk and I told him not to come over."

Derick bellowed, "I know you're in there, Gina! Open up!"

In an unwavering voice, Bob spoke through the door. "She doesn't want to see you right now. Why don't you come back tomorrow, man?"

Derick began yelling. "Who the hell are you? I knew you were screwing around on me, Gina. Let me in, so I can kick his ass!" Derick began pounding on the door relentlessly, forcing Bob to open the door.

Bob grabbed Derick's arm and began to escort him down the hallway. "Just leave the lady alone tonight. Come back when you've slept it off," Bob said in a firm voice.

Derick jerked his arm from Bob's grasp and began towards Gina, who was standing at her doorway.

She whispered, "You're making an ass of yourself, Derick! Don't you remember my partner, Bob? How dare you accuse me of sleeping with him!"

Bob again tried to subdue Derick, who was trying to enter the apartment. They fell to the ground and Derick belted Bob in the face. It was apparent that Bob had put up with this long enough. With one forceful blow to Derick's face, Bob knocked Derick out!

Gina said in an embarrassed tone, "I'm really sorry, Bob. He was way out of line. His temper has caused us many problems in the past and it doesn't seem to be improving."

"What do you want me to do with him?"

"I don't know. What do you think?"

"We could bring him into your apartment until the cop arrives. Then I could take him home," Bob suggested.

"You don't have to do that, Bob. It's not your problem."

"What's the alternative, leaving him here with you alone? That's not going to happen. I also want to take the flowers and card down to the station and log them in as evidence."

Gina graciously said, "Thank you so much. You're always here for me, Bob."

They carried Derick into her apartment and laid him out on the couch. He muttered something every now and then, but it was never rational. Soon after, the officer arrived and Bob helped Derick out of the building. The officer carried down the flowers and put them in Bob's vehicle. Gina watched from the living room window. She never imagined she would be viewing such a sight. Her partner escorting the man she loved away from her building. But did she really love him anymore?

Gina telephoned Christine and told her they didn't catch the man. Gina didn't tell her any details, but said they would talk after she got a good night's sleep. Christine thanked Gina for telling her the truth about Stan and said she planned to confront him with it tomorrow. Gina was curious how Stan would react, but deep down she already knew.

CHAPTER 5

Gina awoke late the next morning, but still felt very tired. The day before had been a stressful one and she relished the thought of a quiet Sunday. She took a shower and was making some breakfast when the phone rang. It was Bob.

"Listen, Gina. I've already called the lab and no one is available to look at the card, so we might as well wait until tomorrow to take it over. You need a day away from the office anyway. Just take it easy and I'll see you at the station tomorrow."

"I guess you're right. Tell Lisa I said 'hello'." They exchanged good-byes and the conversation ended. Gina was left to wonder what she was going to do with her day. She knew she wanted to get out of the apartment, but realized wherever she went, the cop would be following her.

She finished cooking and slowly ate the French toast and sausage. It was very relaxing not to have to rush off to work. As she sat in her bathrobe at the kitchen table, she heard a soft knock at the door. She tiptoed to the door and peered through the peephole. There stood Officer Kimble, the same officer who had guarded her before. Beside him, stood a cheery looking Ted.

The officer said, "This man wants to see you. Is that okay?"

Gina opened the door and answered, "Yes, thank you." She showed Ted into her apartment and closed the door.

"Have a seat, Ted. Let me go get dressed and I'll be right with you." She hurried to her bedroom and changed into jeans and a T-shirt. She returned to find Ted looking at photographs hung on the wall.

She said, "I feel really sorry about what happened to you last night."

He grinned and replied, "I've never been jumped before for trying to talk to a woman. But there's always a first."

They laughed and then Gina said, "You're probably curious why I have a guard again."

Ted admitted, "Somewhat, but I'm sure you're tired of talking about it right now. You can tell me later if you choose. I came over to see if you had any plans today."

She sighed before replying, "I have some unresolved feelings for someone else and don't think it would be the best idea right now."

Ted smiled and said, "I understand you're not ready to date anyone else, but don't think of this as a date. Just think of it as two friends spending some time together."

Deep down, Gina really wanted to get out of the apartment and away from all the chaos. Derick would probably come by again and she needed some time to think about what she wanted to say. Ted seemed like a nice man and the more she got to know him, the more she liked. Ted could tell she was contemplating the offer very seriously.

He tried to lighten the mood by saying, "But then again, if you would rather wait and take your chances with the next guy your partner throws to the pavement, I would understand."

"It feels wonderful to be joking around again. The last few days have been intense."

Ted inquired further, "So does that mean you want to go?"

"I do, but I have an officer assigned to protect me. I don't really think it's necessary, but that's what has been ordered. I plan to talk with the Chief about it tomorrow, but that won't help us now."

"It's not a problem. Don't worry about it, Gina."

"Where are we going, anyway?"

"To a place where you will relax and forget about your troubles. I hope you like animals. I'm taking you to the zoo."

"I haven't been there in ages!" she exclaimed. It sounds like fun. But wait a minute. I think the zoo is closed on Sundays."

He smiled and said, "Yes, it is. How lucky you are to have connections to the animal world."

Gina looked confused and asked, "What do you mean?"

"I work at the city zoo as the assistant manager. I've always loved animals and it's a great place to work. You get to be outside a lot and there isn't much stress."

Gina enthusiastically said, "Give me a few minutes to get ready, okay?"

"Sure, but I hope you're not changing. You may get a little dirty from the animals. Knock on my door when you're ready." He left the apartment and Gina felt glad he had invited her.

A few minutes later, she opened her door and Officer Kimble arose from the chair in the hall. She closed the door behind her and knocked on Ted's door across the hall. She then turned to Kimble and said, "How would you like to go to the zoo with us?"

"My orders are to follow you wherever you go, ma'am."

Ted stepped out and asked, "Are we all ready?"

"Yes," Gina said with a smile.

With Officer Kimble at their heels, they walked to Ted's navy blue Ford Explorer. Ted unlocked the passenger door for her and closed it behind her. He walked around the car and waved at Kimble in the squad car as he got in. As they pulled out of the parking lot, Gina found herself staring at him. She was seeing him in a completely different light.

Finally, she said, "I never had any idea you worked at the zoo."

He joked, "See, we do have something in common. We both work around a bunch of animals." Even though it was corny, she laughed nevertheless.

They arrived at the zoo to find only a few cars in the parking lot. He explained, "There are only a few animal handlers here on Sundays." They got out of the vehicle and Ted suggested, "Why don't I lock your purse in the trunk? You won't be needing it."

"No thanks. My weapon is in there and I want to have it with me."

He answered mildly, "Whatever you think is best." Gina smiled within herself. She couldn't help comparing Ted to Derick. Derick would have had a fit that she wanted the gun.

Ted unlocked the gate to the front entrance and allowed Gina and Officer Kimble to walk in.

Kimble said, "Don't mind me. I'll try to stay out of your way."

Ted locked the gate behind them and led Gina to the first exhibit, which consisted of several different kinds of monkeys. The animals were playful as usual and provided a good show. Gina and Ted walked on, seeing everything from elephants to birds.

Ted said, "Now are you ready for a real treat?"

She smiled with anticipation. "Certainly."

He took her hand and led her to a building. They walked in and she spotted the animal in the large pen to the left of them.

Ted announced, "It's a baby antelope. She's only a few weeks old. There were complications during the labor and the veterinarian couldn't save the mother."

As they stared at the baby antelope, the door to the building opened. A husky looking man in his twenties walked in, carrying a bottle of milk in his right hand. He was taken back by their presence.

"Hello, Mr. Bryant," he said. Gina turned to Ted; she never knew his last name.

Ted responded happily, "Hi, Mike. How's everything going, today?"

"No problems. It's a beautiful spring day and the animals seem to be in good spirits." Ted then introduced Gina and Mike.

Mike asked, "Why is there a police officer walking around out there?"

"I know about him. There's no need to worry about it."

Gina continued to gaze at the little antelope as Ted asked Mike, "Would you mind if we fed her?" Mike looked relieved.

"No, go right ahead. I'm running a little behind today because we're short-handed. Benny is still sick with the flu." Mike handed the bottle of milk to Ted and walked out of the building.

Ted walked up behind Gina and softly tapped her shoulder. He held out the bottle and asked, "Would you like to do the honors?"

She smiled from ear to ear and said, "I'd love to feed her. What's her name?"

"Jenny."

He opened the pen and started to instruct her on how to approach and feed her, but it was unnecessary. Gina stepped into the pen, knelt down, and began calling the antelope, who was watching Gina from the corner. "Come here, girl. It's lunch time."

Jenny made her way to Gina and immediately began drinking the bottle she was holding. She pet Jenny's head gently and continued talking to the animal, almost oblivious that Ted was watching them.

Ted interrupted the meal by saying, "Maybe you missed your true calling, Gina."

She smiled at him and stated, "Maybe so. I grew up on a farm and have always loved animals."

Ted nodded his head in agreement and said, "It shows." By now, Jenny was done with the bottle and began to look sleepy.

"We better leave and let Jenny get some rest," Ted suggested. Gina pet her once more and stepped out of the pen.

They walked out of the building and were blinded by the sun's bright rays. "What a glorious day!" Gina exclaimed.

"It certainly is," Ted replied. "In more ways than one." He smiled at her and she felt a sense of inner peace. She felt at ease with Ted and truly appreciated his easygoing demeanor.

She spotted Officer Kimble standing by the lion's cage and waved at him. He smiled in acknowledgment. Gina and Ted sat down at a bench near the bobcat pen.

She asked, "So is this where you bring all the ladies?"

Ted chuckled and said, "No, you're the first."

She laughed in return and said, "You know I'm a detective and I could ask Mike."

He grinned and answered, "That's true. I will really have to watch myself around you. But what I'm telling you is the truth."

She looked directly into his eyes and agreed, "I believe you."

He stated, "You're a lot of firsts. Not only are you the first woman I've brought here, you're the first who has caused me to be jumped from behind by a man who thought I was going to harm you. I've also never taken a lady out with police protection. Besides all that, you're the first woman in a long time who makes me feel this good." Gina looked away.

Ted reacted intuitively and didn't press the issue any further. "How about some lunch for ourselves now?" he offered.

"That sounds like a good idea. Let's go." She yelled to Kimble, "We're leaving now and will be stopping somewhere for lunch." Kimble nodded his head and began following them out of the zoo.

On the way to the car, Ted asked Gina, "Where would you like to eat?"

"Do you like Italian?" she asked.

He smiled and said, "I love it! I know this great little Italian place over on 53rd Street."

They got into the Explorer and arrived at Rosetti's about fifteen minutes later. Because it was nearly two in the afternoon, most of the lunch crowd had already come and gone. The hostess showed them to a table in the corner. Shortly thereafter, Officer Kimble walked in and was seated at the opposite end of the room.

Gina ordered chicken parmesan with fettuccine noodles and Ted ordered lasagna. They shared a wonderful conversation about their backgrounds, jobs, and hopes for the future. Not once did he pressure her about dating or ask her about Derick. The lunch was delicious and the time passed quickly. When it came time to pay the bill, Gina began reaching for her purse.

Ted stopped her as he said, "This one's on me, no strings attached."

Gina insisted, "Thank you, but I want to pay for my own. I don't want to confuse things."

"Why would there be any confusion? You can pay the next time, and wait until you see the place I pick." She laughed and finally agreed to let Ted pay the bill.

They left the restaurant with Officer Kimble tagging along behind. When they reached their apartments, things became a little awkward. They stood in the hallway which divided their apartments and stared at one another sheepishly. Officer Kimble stood waiting at the other end of the hall.

Gina broke the silence, "Thank you so much for today. I had a marvelous time and did forget my troubles for a little while."

"You're very welcome. The pleasure was all mine."

They smiled as they said good-bye and then entered their own comfort zones. Officer Kimble followed Gina into her apartment and helped her with a quick search before resuming his post.

Gina set her purse down and walked over to her answering machine, which was blinking. It was no surprise to hear a message from Derick.

"Call me. We really need to talk." Then there was a message from Christine.

"Hi, Gina. Please give me a call. I want to tell you what happened with Stan." The third and final message was again from Derick, although he now had a very impatient tone of voice. "Where the hell are you, Gina? I've tried your cell phone, too. Avoiding me is not the answer. If you don't call me back, I'll just come over!"

She sat down on the couch in contemplation. She was glad that she had turned her cell phone off for a few hours. She still didn't feel like talking to Derick, but she knew he meant what he said. He would just come over. She decided to call him and arrange a time to see him tomorrow. She dialed his number and halfheartedly hoped he wasn't there.

He answered, "Hello."

"Hi, Derick."

He immediately grew angry and shouted, "Where the hell have you been all day? I've called you several times. I even called Christine to see if you were there, but she said she didn't know where you were!"

Gina stated firmly, "Calm down or this conversation will end right now. As to where I've been, I didn't realize I had to check in with you first. I just went out with a friend."

Derick asked impatiently, "Gina, if you're seeing someone else, you better tell me now."

"I'm not dating anyone and I don't succumb to threats!"

Derick sighed and then responded, "I love you and want you to be mine."

"You love me? How can you love me today and accuse me of sleeping with Bob last night? You have a warped perception of love. Your jealousy is maddening. I'm not your possession or anyone else's!"

He persisted, "Can't we just get together and talk about this?"

She reluctantly answered, "I'll come by your construction site tomorrow around noon and we'll go to lunch."

In a frustrated tone, he replied, "Tomorrow? Why not today?"

Gina didn't waver, "Take it or leave it." He agreed and hung up.

Gina dialed Christine's number, but she wasn't home. Gina left a message saying she would be home the rest of the evening. She watched a sitcom on television and then took a long, hot bath. It gave her some quiet time to think about everything that was happening.

As she was stepping out of the tub, she heard a knock at the front door. She wrapped a towel around her dripping body and quickly tried to find her bathrobe. But it was nowhere in sight and Officer Kimble was yelling, "Detective Perry, is everything alright in there?"

She shouted in return, "I'll be right there." She hurried to the door and peered through the peephole. It was Christine. Gina opened the door only partially and hid behind it.

"It's okay, Kimble. I was just getting out of the bathtub."

Christine walked in. "I hope you don't mind I just dropped by. I got your message and had to run out for some groceries, anyway."

Gina began to shiver as she held the towel to her wet body. She told Christine, "Make yourself comfortable while I go put on some pajamas."

A few minutes later, Gina came out of the bedroom and went into the kitchen. She said, "I'm making some tea. Would you like some?"

"Yes, please. That sounds good."

Gina walked into the living room holding two mugs of tea and gave one to Christine, who thanked her. Christine began the discussion.

"Gosh, Gina, we have so much to talk about I don't know where to start. I know you were tired and didn't want to talk about it, but did anything else happen last night?"

Gina answered, "No, our guy didn't follow me. However, when I was getting out of my car here, Bob tackled my neighbor, Ted. Ted was walking up to my car just to talk, and Bob thought he was the bad guy."

Christine inquired, "Was Ted hurt?"

"No, he was just a little shaken. Bob thought it was best that I have protection for now, so he got permission to assign an officer to me."

"I think it's wise. It will give me some comfort knowing you're not alone."

Gina changed the subject. "So I hear that Derick called you today."

"Yes, he did. He wanted to know where you were. When I told him that I didn't know, he got rude and said he didn't believe me. What's going on with you two?"

Gina sighed regretfully and said, "I don't think it's going to work out. He came over here drunk last night and saw Bob here with me. He then accused me of sleeping with Bob. He wouldn't leave and then he hit Bob during a struggle. In return, Bob knocked him out cold. He was in such a drunken stupor, it didn't take much. I talked to him on the phone a little while ago and he was irate, demanding to know where I'd been today. I just said I went out with a friend. It's none of his business. I'm meeting with him tomorrow to tell him it's over. I can't take his jealousy any longer."

Christine admitted her feelings. "I think he's becoming overly possessive. He gave me the creeps today on the phone. I never imagined I'd be saying that of him. He's always seemed like such a nice guy. But then again, don't they all seem that way at first?"

Gina asked, "So how did it go with Stan?"

Christine looked away as she said, "Not very well, I'm afraid."

"Well, tell me all about it. What did he say when you confronted him with what I told you?"

Christine hesitated before stating, "Gina, I'm not sure how to tell you this. Obviously, I've known you a lot longer and my loyalty lies with you. But his story was completely different. Stan told me that you came on to him!"

Gina laughed before saying, "You must be joking. I did no such thing. Forget the fact that I wasn't even interested in him. I was dating Derick at the time. You know I'm not that type of person."

"Of course, I know that. I didn't tell him everything you told me about him. I just began by saying you told me the two of you had met before. I asked him why he hadn't told me. Stan must have realized you had told me of his advances, because then he said you made advances toward him. He told me on the last occasion, you unbuttoned your shirt, pulled him against your body, and kissed him forcefully. He said you were interrupted by another worker and you left."

Gina began laughing uncontrollably and Christine joined in. Finally, Christine said, "He's really mad at you, Gina. I told him you said he was the aggressor. He said it was all a lie. He claimed he didn't tell me about it because we were good friends and he didn't want to embarrass you."

Gina inquired, "So how did you leave things with him?"

"I told him I needed some time to think it all over. I knew I didn't want to see him again, but I wanted to give him some time to cool off before I told him. As much as I liked him and wanted to believe him, I just couldn't believe his story. The vision of you coming on to him like that at a construction site made me giggle."

Gina tried to console her, "I'm sorry it had to end like this. I know how much you wanted a relationship."

Christine rolled her eyes. "Oh well, so where were you today?"

Gina smiled and answered, "It's not what you think. Ted and I went to the zoo and then to lunch. He's the assistant manager at the zoo, so we were able to see the animals even though it was closed to the public. I even got to feed a baby antelope!"

Christine asked enthusiastically, "And what about Ted?"

Gina replied jokingly, "No, he fed himself."

They laughed for a moment before Christine asked, "Why are you being evasive about him?"

"Because I don't know how I feel about him. I had a wonderful time with him. He is very gentle, caring, and has a great sense of humor. He wants to date me, but he knows I have unresolved feelings for Derick and he hasn't pressed the issue."

"So what's the problem?" Christine asked.

"I don't want to date him just because I'm on the rebound from Derick. I want my motivations to be genuine."

Christine laughed and said, "While you're analyzing everything to death, some other woman may try her luck with Ted. I'm available once again!"

Gina giggled and said, "I get your point, Christine. I just don't want to rush into anything."

Christine asked, "Do you have any new leads on who's stalking you?"

Gina let out a sigh. "No, not really. Bob and I are going to work on it more this week. Maybe we'll be able to develop more clues as to the suspect's identity. The problem is Bob and I have differing opinions about who is involved. Bob thinks it's all connected to Dwayne Timbers, the man on trial for murdering his girlfriend. He did threaten me countless times and has friends on the outside, but I just don't think it's him. The man who attacked me seemed to know me somehow. It seemed more personal than what one of Timber's friends could do. I don't know how to explain it. It's just a gut feeling."

"Then who do you think did it?" Christine asked.

"I'm unsure, but I tend to lean more towards another criminal who I've investigated. Do you remember when I got in trouble for following a guy by the name of John Utik, whom I and everyone else believed raped that waitress?"

"Yes, I remember. It was in all the papers. He got an attorney and filed a harassment suit against you and the police department. And didn't you have to go before a judge for some reason?"

"Yes, I did because of the lawsuit. It was Judge Slocum who issued a restraining order against me to stay away from Utik."

Christine asked, "Was that the judge who belittled you in his office and told you that you had better learn to respect the law?"

"Yes, that's him alright. He made me feel completely worthless. I hope I never have any further meetings with him in his chambers. He's not someone you would want to cross. Anyway, I think Utik may have been the one who attacked me. He's the same physical description and expressed a deep hatred towards me."

Christine's voice rose, "So what are you going to do?"

Gina paused and then said, "We'll do some more interviews and try to develop new leads to pursue. Who knows? Maybe it's neither of these men, but they are the most likely choices. Police work can be very interesting. Nothing is impossible. You just have to keep digging until you find what you're looking for."

Christine said, "John Utik."

"No, the truth, even if it's not the suspect you believed it would be."

Christine stood up and said, "I'd better get going. Take care of yourself and let me know how it goes with Derick tomorrow." Gina nodded her head and walked Christine to the door.

Gina opened the door to find Officer Kimble had been relieved. She said "hello" to the new officer as Christine walked to the elevator. She then went back into her apartment and locked the door behind her.

CHAPTER 6

Gina slept well that night and hurried off to work the next morning. Just before 8 AM, she arrived at the station to find Bob hovering over his desk reviewing old files. Gina was bright, "Good morning, Bob."

"Good morning. I hope you don't mind, but I already took the flowers and card over to the lab. Chief Buchanon was in a bad mood and was yelling at everyone over minor details. I thought it would be a good time to get out of the office."

Gina answered, "I understand. Did they find anything at the lab?"

He shook his head and said, "The only fingerprints on the card were yours and Christine's. I already ran them through the computer. They couldn't get any prints off of the tissue paper covering the flowers."

Gina sighed in disappointment and asked, "So where does that leave us?"

He shrugged. "Square one," he said. Bob then leaned back in his chair and stared mysteriously at Gina.

"What?" she asked.

"Have you ever thought maybe we're focusing too much on Timbers and Utik?"

"Who else do you have in mind?"

Bob questioned, "What about someone from your personal life?"

Gina muttered, "Like who?"

"You tell me. Can you think of anyone who would want to get back at you, maybe an old boyfriend?"

She paused for a moment while thinking and then said, "No, I can't think of anyone who would do something like this."

Bob stated firmly, "Well, you let me know if anyone comes to mind."

Logan walked over to Gina's desk and reported, "I finally got in touch with Timbers' former probation officer, Denise Steidman. She and her husband were out of town Saturday and came back late last night. She's on her way here. Would you like to sit in?"

Gina quickly answered, "Yes, I would. Let me know when she gets here." Gina turned to Bob and smiled while saying, "It looks like we may turn up some information which could prove Timbers was involved, like you said. Maybe he's hired his friends to do a couple different jobs."

Bob glanced up from the paperwork and said, "I've been reviewing the notes regarding the attacks on Laura Adams, Shirley Jenson, and you. I can't find a link between the three of you. What do a firefighter, waitress, and detective have in common? Maybe there is no link and these acts were committed by different men. And how does this current attempt involving Denise Steidman fit into the picture?"

A determined Gina answered, "I can't answer that right now. But I'll let you know when I figure it out."

Logan came over and said, "Denise Steidman is waiting in the interview room." Gina got up and followed him to the room. They walked through the doorway and the two women shook hands.

Steidman smiled and said, "It's nice to see you again, Gina."

"Likewise, Denise. How have you been doing?"

"Oh, fine. I've just been busy as usual trying to keep up with my caseload. How can I help the two of you?" Steidman asked.

Logan began the questioning. "Mrs. Steidman, we would like to ask you a few questions about Dwayne Timbers."

She replied in a friendly manner. "First of all, please call me Denise. Secondly, I'm curious why you want to ask me questions about him when I've already testified at his trial about the murder of his girlfriend."

Logan inquired, "Denise, do you think Timbers would hold a grudge to the point he would hire someone on the outside to harm those he disliked?"

"That's a very interesting question. Having been his probation officer, I got to know him a little more than I would have liked. He's a very cunning and manipulative man. I would say he's capable of anything. Why do you ask?"

Logan glanced at Gina and then looked back at Denise. He asked, "Do you think it's likely that Timbers hired someone to break into your home Friday night to harm you?"

Denise looked surprised and responded, "I don't know. It could have been anyone. An officer talked to me after my neighbor called 911 Friday night. The officer didn't mention anything about Timbers being involved. What makes you think so?"

Gina interjected, "We have no proof he was involved. Denise, a man broke into my apartment on Thursday night and threatened me with a knife. He had me pinned down on the floor when a friend of mine knocked on the door and scared him away. I didn't get a good look at the man because he wore a ski mask. Since that night, I've received threatening notes. Someone is stalking me and I'm trying to determine who it is. Timbers is just a possibility at this point, nothing more. But when I found out someone had tried to break into your home on the next night, I wondered if there was a connection."

Denise was stunned. "Gina, I'm so glad you're alright. What can I do to help you?"

"I just need to know if Timbers ever threatened you."

Denise responded, "No, never openly. He always gave me the creeps, but so do a lot of other probationers."

Gina questioned her further. "Who can you recall of Timbers' friends and relatives who would fit this description?" Gina slid a piece of paper across the table to Denise. On the paper, was the physical description of her attacker.

Denise stared intensely at the description and replied, "He and his cousin are really close, but his cousin is much shorter than this. Dwayne has a lot of friends. Many could fit this build. I could review my reports and get back with you."

Logan added, "We would appreciate it."

Gina said, "He may be linked with other attacks as well. So it's urgent we act upon this quickly. But again, let me reemphasize. There is no direct proof Timbers is behind all of this."

Denise nodded in acknowledgment. "I understand. Thanks for letting me know about this. I'll get back with you as soon as possible."

As Denise began to leave the room, Gina stopped her. "One other thing, would you like to have an officer assigned to you until this blows over? Since I received the second note, Bob insisted I have protection. He assigned an officer to me when I'm off duty. It's up to you, Denise."

Denise smiled and said, "Thanks, but I don't think that will be necessary. It would only worry my husband. He's never wanted me to be a probation officer and this would only strengthen his argument. Besides, we have no real reason to believe this guy will return. I haven't received any threats of any kind. If I do, then I'll take you up on your offer."

Gina said in parting, "Take care, Denise."

"You too, Gina." Denise then looked at Detective Logan and said, "It was nice to meet you."

He shook her hand and said, "Same here, Denise."

Gina and Logan walked over to Bob, who was still sitting at his desk. They relayed what had transpired and Logan said, "Let me know if you develop anything. I have to go talk with someone on a different case. See you later!" Bob and Gina said good-bye and Logan left the station.

Bob said, "I have plans for an early lunch today."

Gina asked, "Are you finally going to take out your better half?"

He laughed and said, "Yes, Lisa hasn't seemed herself lately and I don't know what's wrong. I thought I would surprise her by going to her office and taking her out for lunch. What do you think?"

"It sounds wonderful. I'm sure she would love the gesture."

He continued, "Lisa just seems distant lately and I don't know what to do. I know I'm not as romantic as some husbands, but if that's what she needs, I'm willing to try harder."

Gina inquired, "When are you leaving?"

"Right now, I guess. I'm not even sure if it's a good idea. Lisa may even have plans to go somewhere with her co-workers on her lunch hour."

Gina smiled supportively and stated, "I'm certain she would rather go to lunch with her dashing husband than with the other secretaries. She'll be very happy to see you!"

He muttered, "I don't know. It's just so unlike me."

"That's exactly why she'll appreciate it even more! I'm headed in that direction, do you want me to drop you off and Lisa can give you a ride back?"

"Sure, that sounds like a good idea."

The drive over was a fairly quiet one, as Bob seemed lost in thought. Gina commented, "The weather sure has been beautiful lately. Even though it's only April, it feels like summer is already here." Bob didn't make a sound. It was apparent to Gina there was more going on with his marriage than she had been told. But she didn't want to pressure him now. He would tell her about it when he was ready.

They parked on the street in front of Lisa's office building. Gina asked, "Do you want me to wait here, just in case she's already gone to lunch?"

"Yeah, that's a good idea."

He stepped out and swung the car door closed. Gina watched as he walked into the building. She sat restlessly in the car, wondering how her own lunch with Derick would turn out. She had finally gotten up the courage to tell him it wasn't going to work out between them. Today was the day he was going to be told.

Only a short time elapsed before Gina spotted Bob walking quickly out of the building. He was obviously upset. He got into the car and slammed the door closed.

Bob looked at Gina and said in a daze, "I think Lisa's having an affair."

Gina was flabbergasted and asked, "Why would you think that?"

"They told me she just left about a half hour ago and took the rest of the day off. Nobody knew where she was going."

Gina shook her head and said, "Bob, that doesn't mean she's having an affair."

"Alright, then you tell me why she would be so secretive. She didn't tell me she was taking part of the day off, nor did she tell her co-workers."

Finally, Gina asked, "Do you have any other reasons to make you so suspicious of Lisa?"

"She's just been very distant all the time and doesn't seem to be interested in me anymore."

Gina tried to convince him that he was jumping to conclusions. "Look, I'm sure there's a logical explanation for all of this. Lisa loves you dearly and wouldn't do that to you, Bob."

He demanded, "Just take me back to the station. I don't want to talk about this any longer."

Gina complied and dropped him off at the station. She knew he needed some time alone. She told him she had plans for lunch, but would return to the station in an hour or so.

The drive to the construction site seemed like a long one. At last, she pulled into the lot designated as Reed and Meyers, Incorporated. She got out of the car and nervously walked through the construction zone. She received the usual catcalls and invasive jeers. One man yelled, "Hey baby, why don't you and me hammer together?" Another yelled at the man, "Leave that one alone; that's Richards' woman!" Now she remembered why she hated coming here. But she didn't want Derick to come over to her apartment. She wanted to end this as cleanly as possible. If they were at home, he would refuse to leave. This way, they could have lunch together and would have to get back to work.

After walking through several areas, she saw Derick working on a doorframe. She walked up behind him and said, "Hello, Derick." He turned towards her and smiled.

"Hi, Gina. Just let me finish this one thing and I'll be ready to go to lunch."

She waited patiently for a few minutes, noticing everyone seemed to be staring at her. Then she saw Stan and had an uneasy feeling in her stomach. He spotted her and immediately began towards her.

Stan got in Gina's face and yelled, "Where do you get off trying to turn Christine against me?"

Derick was on him in a flash; he pushed Stan to the floor. "Stay away from her!" Stan got free, jumped to his feet, and glared at Derick.

"This doesn't involve you, Richards. I just want to talk to her," Stan said.

Derick looked at Gina and asked, "Do you want to talk to him?"

Gina glanced at Stan and said resolutely, "I only told Christine the truth. It's her decision what she chooses to do. I have nothing more to say to you, Stan."

With that, Derick threw down his hammer and said, "Let's go to lunch, Gina." Stan glowered at them as they left the construction area.

Gina and Derick walked to his pickup and got in. He stated, "There's a burger joint a couple blocks away."

"That's fine."

Derick looked curiously at her and asked, "What was all that about with Masterson?"

"It was nothing, really. He and Christine have been dating and I told her how he had treated me those times. Now, Christine doesn't want to see him anymore and he's mad at me."

He said firmly, "Just stay away from him, Gina. I don't trust him."

They parked and walked into the restaurant. They were seated and given their menus. Gina stared at him, hoping she would be able to go through with her intentions.

"What's wrong?" he asked.

She took a deep breath and told him, "I would never want to hurt you, Derick. You know that. But it's imperative I be honest with you. I don't think it's going to work out between us."

"Why not? You know I would do anything for you."

The waitress interrupted their conversation. "What can I get you?"

He quickly answered, "I'll have the special."

Gina said, "I'll have the same, please."

The waitress collected their menus and went to the kitchen. Derick and Gina held hands across the table and continued their discussion.

He asked, "What's his name?"

"Whose name?"

He was bristling, "Don't pretend you don't know what I'm talking about! There must be another man in your life."

She shook her head and said, "I haven't dated anyone else. I just feel you and I are too different and are not meant for one another. I do have a male friend, but we haven't dated."

He asked vehemently, "What does this other guy have that I don't have?"

She looked away and then said, "I told you! He's just a friend."

Derick began to raise his voice, "Whatever! Say what you want to say. I won't allow you to see him again!"

Gina pulled her hand from his grasp and shouted, "You won't allow me to see him? Who the hell do you think you are? I tried to be civil about this, but I refuse to put up with your jealous attitude any longer. It's definitely over between us! Don't come by or call me again!" Gina grabbed her purse and stormed out of the restaurant, leaving a room full of people gaping at Derick.

She walked the few blocks to her car and sped away from the construction site. She couldn't believe the nerve of that man! To think that he believed he could control her like that! In some ways, it made the breakup much easier. She knew she could never stay with a man who didn't respect her independence.

She arrived at the station to find Bob with his head down on his desk. She walked up behind him and placed her hand on his shoulder. He looked up and asked, "How was your lunch?"

"Not too good, I'm afraid. But I don't want to bother you with it."

Bob quickly added, "Actually, I'd like to hear about it. Maybe it would help to know everyone else has personal problems, too. Why don't we get out of here and you can tell me about it in the car?"

"Fine. Where are we going?"

"Let's go," he muttered. He abruptly put on his jacket and headed for the door, with Gina hurrying to catch up.

They got into the car and with Bob driving, left the police station. It was obvious to Gina he knew where he was going, so she didn't ask him about it further. He broke the silence by inquiring, "So what happened with your lunch date?"

She stared out the window while saying, "I told Derick I didn't want to see him anymore. He became upset and thought I was dating someone else. I told him I had a male friend and he said he wouldn't allow me to see my friend again. Can you believe his audacity?"

Bob smiled and said, "Actually, I can. He's always seemed like a very domineering man and I wondered how the two of you managed to get along."

"Why didn't you ever say anything to me about it?"

Bob laughed and answered, "Because you're a very strong willed woman and wouldn't have wanted to hear it. I knew you would find out on your own."

She laughed and said, "I guess you're right. It just took me longer than you to see through his bullshit."

Gina looked out the window and noticed they were headed towards Bob's house. She asked excitedly, "Bob, where are we going?"

He said stoically, "I have to know if Lisa's there with someone. I must find out the truth. If the Chief hadn't called me into his office for a case update, I would have left sooner. I just finished talking with him when you got back."

"You're going about this all wrong. Remember how idiotic Derick looked when he accused me of sleeping with you? That's how you'll look if you run in the house accusing Lisa of something that isn't true."

Undaunted, Bob kept driving and turned onto his street. As they neared his house, he spotted an unfamiliar car parked in front of his house. "See, what did I tell you?"

Gina shook her head and said adamantly, "That doesn't mean anything, Bob. That car could belong to anyone. Don't make a fool of yourself!"

Bob was already halfway out of the car when he screamed hastily, "Someone's going to pay!"

Gina yelled, "Give me your weapon!" He ignored her and tore into the house. She ran in behind him.

As they stormed down the hallway leading to the bedroom, Lisa stepped into the hallway from the bedroom. She was startled to see them and asked, "What's going on?"

Before Bob could respond, Gina did. "We stopped by your office to see if you wanted to go to lunch. We found out you had taken the rest of the day off and got worried. We thought you might not be feeling well and came here to see if you were okay."

"Oh. I'm fine. I'm sorry you had to come all the way over here."

Bob asked, "So why did you come home?"

Lisa paused before saying, "Well, I had a disagreement with my supervisor and had to get out of the office for awhile."

It was not a very convincing statement and even Gina began to theorize what was really going on. Before any further questions could be asked about it, Lisa stated, "I'd really rather not talk about it right now." Gina still saw Bob glancing around the house.

Bob then said, "Oh, Gina, you haven't seen our bedroom since we redecorated it. Why don't you show it to her, Lisa?"

Lisa quickly answered, "It's really a mess right now. How about another time?"

Gina replied, "That would be fine." But Bob was already walking in that direction. He walked into the bedroom with the two women following. Gina was very apprehensive.

The room was simply a mess. The bed hadn't been made and there were various articles of women's clothing strewn about the floor.

Lisa looked embarrassed and said, "I was running late for work this morning and didn't have time to straighten up."

A stunned Bob looked on as Gina said, "Oh, don't worry about it. My place isn't the most tidy, either. I love the new border and decor, Lisa."

"Thank you," Lisa answered. Lisa then gave Bob the evil eye for bringing Gina into a messy room.

Gina smiled at Bob and said, "I'll give you two a moment alone. I'll wait outside." As she turned to exit the bedroom, Lisa grabbed her arm.

"I haven't seen you since you were attacked. How are you doing?"

"Okay, thanks." They all walked into the living room and Gina headed for the front door.

Lisa told Bob, "There was a man here a little while ago who was giving free estimates on roofing. His car's still out front." Gina smiled at Bob, but said nothing. As they glanced at the car, they saw a man exiting the house across the street with a clipboard in hand.

Lisa asked Bob, "Honey, why don't you just talk to him about it? It may come in handy later on."

Bob looked bewildered and so relieved too, he would have done anything she asked. If she wanted him to talk to a roofing man, then that's what he would do. He stepped outside and walked across the street. Gina and Lisa watched as the two men shook hands and began a conversation. Gina started to walk out the door, but was stopped by Lisa's words.

"Gina, I need to talk to you. Do you have a minute?"

Gina grinned and said, "You have no interest in getting a new roof, do you?"

"No, I just wanted to get Bob out of the house for a few minutes."

Lisa had a look of concern in her eyes that scared Gina. Gina grabbed her hand and asked, "Is everything alright?" Lisa sat down on the couch and Gina followed.

"I need your opinion on something. You've always been very open with me, Gina, and I need that now."

Gina swallowed hard and answered, "Okay. What is it?"

Lisa admitted, "I didn't have an argument with my supervisor. That's not why I left work."

"If that wasn't the reason, why did you leave?"

Lisa took a deep breath. "I had an appointment with my doctor."

With fear in her voice, Gina asked "Are you okay?"

"Yes, I'm okay. I'm sorry. I didn't mean to worry you like that. The fact is I'm pregnant." Before she could say another word, Gina gave her a big hug.

"I'm so happy for you!" It became obvious that Lisa did not share in her enthusiasm. Gina asked, "Do you not want to have another child?"

Lisa exclaimed, "I would love to have another child! Kyle will be going away to college next year. It would be wonderful to have another baby. It's Bob I'm worried about. He's always talking about how wonderful it will be when we have time to ourselves."

Gina assured her, "Bob would love to have another child. Sure, he'll be surprised, but he'll adapt. He loves you very much, Lisa."

"I didn't tell him I was going to the doctor's because I wanted to be sure. I didn't want to lie to him. I just needed some time to figure things out. You really think he'll be happy about this?"

Gina grinned widely and said, "I'm sure of it. You should tell him right away."

"I'll tell him tonight over a romantic dinner!" Lisa exclaimed.

As they embraced, the door swung open and in walked Bob. He mumbled, "I can't believe the cost of a new roof these days. I think we can wait awhile for one, Lisa."

Lisa smiled at Bob and said, "Whatever you think is best, honey."

Gina walked to the door and said good-bye to Lisa. As Gina headed for the car, Bob and Lisa exchanged a kiss on the porch. He walked to the car a happy man. Gina beamed within herself, for she knew he was about to become even happier.

He got into the car and smiled gratefully at Gina. "I want to thank you for stopping me from making a big mistake in there, Gina."

"What are partners for?"

"Apparently for helping me out with my insecurities. I'm so relieved that I was wrong about Lisa. I couldn't be more ecstatic." Gina smiled, but said not a word!

CHAPTER 7

Gina and Bob drove back to the station and spent the rest of the afternoon doing paperwork which Chief Buchanon ordered be done before they leave. It seemed trivial to them, but it was the gleam in management's eyes. It was the way they measured the department's production, which in turn, measured the Chief himself.

Gina also spoke to Chief Buchanon about having an officer assigned to her while she was off duty. Despite her opinion that it was unnecessary, he told her that it would continue whenever she was at her apartment. If she went out in public, one of the detectives would follow her. Bob would oversee the logistics.

Gina had hoped to hear from Denise Steidman by the day's end. It would be very useful to have a list of names of Timbers' friends who would match the general physical description. But upon completion of the tedious paperwork, Gina hadn't heard from her. It was already 6 PM, so she decided to go home. She wished Bob a good evening and left the station.

She arrived home to find a message on her answering machine from Christine. Stan had telephoned Christine and was very upset about everything. He felt Gina was trying to break them up and he was insistent it wouldn't work.

Gina was very relieved when the machine showed no other messages. She didn't want to deal with Derick anymore. She just wanted him to get over it and move on. She was very proud of how she handled him today. She said what she wanted to say and didn't waver. She felt a rush of freedom flow through her body as never before. It now felt odd that she had been confused about whether she wanted to date him. She saw his true colors and everything was crystal clear. She could only hope other issues in her life would transcend as quickly.

She picked up the phone and called Christine, who was happy to hear from her. "Gina, Stan won't stop calling me. I just want him to leave me alone! Is that too much to ask?"

"Of course not," Gina replied.

"Well, what am I supposed to do now?"

Gina said firmly, "Just make it clear to him you don't want to have any further contact with him. Tell him if he won't leave you alone, you'll be forced to call the police and file a complaint."

After a moment of silence, Christine responded. "Do you think that will work?"

"There's only one way to find out. Has Stan threatened you in any way?"

"No, do you think he will?"

Gina carefully chose her words before she spoke. "It's always better to be prepared, right? Let me know if you hear from him again." They exchanged good-byes and hung up.

Gina headed for the kitchen, happy her only dilemma right now was what she would have for dinner. With all of the commotion that had been going on, she hadn't had time to go grocery shopping. Her refrigerator showed only a lot of empty space. She was contemplating going out to eat when she heard a knock at the door.

The officer announced, "Your neighbor, Ted, would like to see you."

She opened the door to find Ted standing beside the officer. "It's alright," she said. "Come on in, Ted."

She invited him to have a seat in the living room, which he did. She sat down at the other end of the couch and asked him, "How was your day?"

"It went pretty well. And yours?"

She smiled and said, "Today was a turning point for me."

"In what way?"

Gina paused before replying, "I stood up to Derick, my ex-boyfriend. We broke up about a month ago, but were considering getting back together. After much contemplation, I realized he was not the man I was searching for and I told him it was over."

Ted could not hide his happiness. A grin developed on his face and his eyes beamed with delight as he inquired, "Exactly what kind of man are you looking for?"

"Someone who can respect my independence and love me for who I am. He also must have control of his temper and not be the jealous type."

Ted moved closer towards her on the couch and held her hand. Gina's pulse raced. She was growing very fond of him and he was even becoming more attractive the longer she knew him. It wasn't that he had been unattractive. Until now, he just looked like the average man. But that was then and things were changing. His sincerity and gentle ways were winning a place in her heart, a place never occupied by Derick. She wanted to get to know him better, but was unsure if this was the right time.

Her thoughts were quickly interrupted by the sound of Ted's voice. "Well, when you're ready for that man, let me know. I'm sure I know someone who could fit the bill. In the meantime, how would you like to come over to my place for dinner?"

Gina couldn't veil her enthusiasm, "I would love to." Her appreciation of him just deepened. Other men would have jumped on the situation, but not Ted.

He said, "Good. It's nothing fancy. I was just going to cook some burgers on the patio grill. I'm starving. Are you ready to go or do you want to come over in a few minutes?" She glanced down at what she was wearing, a dressy beige pant suit.

"Just let me change and I'll be right over."

"No problem, take your time," he answered.

She walked him to the door and locked it behind him. She hurriedly changed into jeans, a casual shirt, and a pair of Nikes. She didn't feel like wearing a shoulder holster, so she just tucked her gun in the back of her waistband. She then clipped her cell phone onto her belt. While doing so, her other phone began to ring. She started to pick up, but decided to let the answering machine get it. Just as she expected, it was Derick. He wanted to meet again and settle things. She thought, What's left to be settled?

She was glad she hadn't answered the phone. She was truly enjoying Ted's company and did not want Derick, or anything else, to spoil the evening. She opened the door to the hallway and told the officer on guard she would be in the apartment across the hall. She knocked on Ted's door and she heard him shout, "Come on in! The door's open!"

As she opened the door and walked in, her eyes quickly scanned the apartment. The furniture was nice, as were the decorations. The walls were covered with paintings of all kinds of animals. As she was looking at some animal pictures on a bookcase in the living room, Ted stepped in from the patio with a spatula in hand. The wonderful aroma of charbroiled hamburgers permeated the living room.

He asked, "So what do you think of those photographs?"

She answered in an astonished tone, "Did you take these pictures yourself?" He smiled and she knew it was true. "I think you did a wonderful job. It doesn't look like a lot of these pictures were taken of animals in captivity."

He said, "No, I like to go hiking and camping. I see a lot of wildlife in the woods and try to get some good shots out there."

Gina held up a photograph of a bear as she asked, "How did you get so close to this one?"

Ted laughed as he said, "It was a very powerful zoom lens."

He walked to the kitchen and got a bottle of Heinz barbecue sauce from the refrigerator. He then went out to the patio and she followed. As he tended to the grill, she stared off towards the pool below them.

She commented, "You're lucky to have the view on this side. When I moved in, no apartments were available that overlooked the pool and grounds."

He smiled in agreement before asking, "Do you like to swim? I don't recall seeing you down there last summer."

"Yes, I like to swim, but it's always so crowded down there that I don't go much. I like more peaceful settings."

In no time at all, the burgers were cooked to perfection and they ate dinner inside. Thoughts continued to race through Gina's mind. Was she truly beginning to have feelings for this man or was she simply on the rebound from Derick? She was unsure. After all, they had really broken up about a month ago, not today. Maybe it was time she move on. She finally knew Derick was a part of her past and not her future. And before her, sat a very caring man who seemed to come along at just the right time. Or did he?

Her contemplations were interrupted by Ted's sincere voice, "Is everything okay, Gina? You seem a little quiet."

She smiled as she replied, "I'm sorry. I just have a lot on my mind."

He inquired, "Regarding your work?"

She glanced away as she said, "Yeah, something like that." She didn't want him to know of her feelings yet. After all, she was still uncertain how she felt herself. She wanted to see how things developed on their own.

The meal ended and she arose to help him with the dishes. "These can wait," he said, as he took her hand and led her to the patio. It was now dark outside and a full moon shone down upon them. They stood at the railing and stared dreamily up at the sky. Ted turned to her and said, "I want you to know how much I enjoy your company, whether it be on a platonic basis or more."

Gina smiled. "I enjoy being with you, too."

They gazed into one another's eyes and he pulled her closer to him. In Gina's mind, the world seemed to stand still momentarily. Ted leaned down to kiss her, but in that split second, they were interrupted by the sound of Gina's cell phone ringing.

They parted rather abruptly as she looked at the phone number displayed on the screen. It was Bob's cell phone number. She thought Lisa must have told him about the pregnancy and he wanted to share the news. She apologized to Ted for the interruption and took the call.

In an anxious tone of voice, Bob asked, "Gina, where are you?"

"I'm across the hall at my neighbor's. Why?"

He hastily informed, "There's been another attack. Only this time he killed her." She blanched and a knot began to form in her stomach. Bob continued, "I'll pick you up outside your apartment in five minutes. Your place is on the way."

She turned to Ted, who knew something was wrong. "I'm sorry, Ted, but I have to go. A woman has been murdered. I'll talk to you later."

She hastily left his apartment, told the officer in the hallway what had happened, and got her purse from her apartment. She ran down the hallway to the elevator, with the officer following closely behind. The ride down in the elevator seemed like an eternity. As the doors opened, she saw Bob's vehicle pull into the lot outside. She hurried to the car and jumped in.

The officer ran to Bob's side of the car and asked, "What's the address? I can lead and clear traffic for you."

"4804 Rosemont," Bob replied. The officer ran to his patrol car and led the way.

Gina said, "That address sounds familiar to me. Does it to you, Bob?"

"No. We should be there in just a couple minutes, though. It helps to have a patrol car leading the way." He pointed to the flashing light mounted on the dash and said, "This light doesn't get as much attention."

A few minutes later, they arrived at 4804 Rosemont. Police vehicles were parked at odd angles and curious neighbors gawked at all the activity. Gina and Bob walked to the front door, being greeted by officers who knew them.

One yelled, "The body is upstairs in the master bedroom." As they climbed the stairs, Gina quickly put on a pair of plastic gloves. Bob did the same.

They walked into the bedroom, where a police photographer was taking pictures of the horrific scene. A nude woman lay face down in a pool of blood on the bed. Her face was covered by her hair and matted blood. Her torn clothing was strewn all over the floor. The room was in complete disarray. Lamps lay broken on the carpet, the dresser mirror was shattered, and paintings were ripped from the wall. This woman had fought for her life.

Bob asked, "Who was the first officer at the scene?"

Officer Brooks stepped forward and announced, "I was and the scene has been secured."

Gina piped in, "Who found the body?"

Officer Brooks replied, "A friend of hers. She's downstairs."

The photographer stopped taking pictures and said, "I have enough shots of the body." Gina slowly walked towards the bed and extended her hand towards the body.

While doing so, she asked, "Is this how she was found?"

Officer Brooks answered, "Yes, Detective Perry." Gina gently pulled the woman's hair away from her face. Gina's eyes dilated and she gasped for breath.

She turned to Bob, "This is Denise Steidman! She was Dwayne Timbers' former probation officer!"

Bob walked over and stood by Gina's side, as she stared at the body. Gina yelled at the officers standing in the doorway. "Go check for signs of forced entry and prints downstairs!"

Bob reached for Steidman's bare shoulder to turn the body over, but Gina grabbed his arm. With saddened eyes and a frown on her face, she said, "Let me do this."

Bob nodded in agreement and Gina gently touched the cold shoulders of Denise Steidman. She rolled the body over only to find a more ghastly sight. The abdomen had been torn to shreds by a knife and Gina gasped at the sight of Steidman's chest. The attacker had etched a message into the skin, apparently by the knife blade. Blood lay in the crevices of the letterings which read, "G I N A!"

Fighting revulsion, her stomach quivering, Gina looked away. Bob pulled her towards him and gave her a compassionate hug. Officer Brooks asked in astonishment, "Do you know who did this?"

Gina answered in a trembling voice, "No, but I'll find out. And when I do, he'll know he's no longer in control!"

Flashes of photography lit up the bedroom as pictures were taken of the letters carved in the victim's chest. Gina and Bob searched the room for further clues, but found nothing left by the attacker. The coroner, Ralph Faraday, arrived and officially declared Denise Steidman was dead. This had always seemed very strange to Gina. No matter how obvious it was the victim was dead, it wasn't official until Faraday said so. He was a nice enough man. He just seemed overly interested by the destruction of the human body. But he had a very difficult job and was among the best in his field.

Faraday did a precursory survey of the body and informed, "A lot of those cuts are superficial, but a few of them are very deep, causing severe trauma. It looks like the killer used a knife with some type of jagged edge. It appears she was sexually assaulted, but I'll have more details after the autopsy. Come by my office tomorrow afternoon and I'll go over the results with you."

Gina and Bob nodded in agreement as the body was placed in a bag on a stretcher. Other detectives continued to search the house for prints or any other pieces of evidence, as Gina and Bob followed behind the stretcher down the stairway. A delirious woman rushed from the living room to the stretcher, which was now being rolled towards the front door. She tried to unzip the bag, but was obstructed by officers, who held her back as the lifeless body of her friend was escorted outside. She continued to fight with the officers, while sobbing uncontrollably. Gina intervened by motioning to the two male officers to let the woman go.

Gina slowly walked up to the dazed woman and their eyes met. Gina took a step forward and grasped the woman's hand. The woman immediately collapsed against Gina and Gina comforted her shuddering body. Bob began to ask the woman a question, but was cut off by a wicked glare from Gina. The woman continued to sob as Gina held her closely. After what seemed like an eternity to Bob, but was realistically only a minute, Gina's soft voice broke the silence.

"Why don't we go sit down in the living room?"

She guided the woman into the living room and sat down beside her on the couch. The woman was still in shock and began to hyperventilate. Gina quickly arose from the couch and sat down on the coffee table directly facing her. She gently clutched the woman's shoulders and spoke calmly. "Look at me. You're going to be fine. You just need to calm down. Take a deep breath and exhale slowly. Follow me." Bob watched as both women breathed laboriously. Slowly, the woman began to catch her breath.

Gina seized the moment and introduced herself. "My name is Gina Perry. I'm a detective with the police department. What's your name?"

In between shallow whimpers, the woman said, "Valerie Bruster." Gina reached across the coffee table for a Kleenex and offered it to Valerie.

Gina began, "I know this is extremely difficult for you, but I have to ask you a few questions, Valerie." There was no response.

"How long have you known Denise?" Gina asked.

"We were roommates in college and have remained close friends ever since," Valerie answered. "I can't believe she's gone!"

Valerie leaned forward and fell into Gina's lap, crying profusely once again. Gina hugged her and tried to calm her down, but to no avail.

Gina suggested, "Why don't I go get a glass of water for you?" Gina began to move, but was held down by Valerie's tight grasp.

"Please don't leave me!" Valerie wailed.

"Okay, I'll stay. Bob, could you get her a glass of water, please?" Bob turned and was off to the kitchen.

Gina moved to the couch and cradled Valerie's grief stricken body. Gina whispered softly, "It's okay. Let it all out. I'm not going anywhere."

Gina felt Valerie's pain wholeheartedly. Her mind wandered back to the night she was told her parents and siblings were killed in the car accident. She knew what it was like to be overwhelmed by shock and feelings of despair. It was as if a large piece of her soul had been ripped out, never to be replaced. Upon hearing of the accident, she had cried non-stop for hours while Christine held her. Showing her emotions openly was very unlike Gina prior to the accident, but things had changed since then. Now, it was as if a faucet to her emotions had been irreversibly opened. She wished she could change it, but that was not possible.

Gina's retrospection was awakened by Valerie's sniffles against her chest. She stroked Valerie's head softly. Bob returned with a glass of water and set it down on the coffee table in front of the two women. Upon hearing him, Valerie pulled away from Gina and began to apologize. "I'm sorry I lost it. I'm really not like this. I just can't believe anyone would do this to Denise!"

Gina sighed, "You reacted like any other person would in the same situation." Noting the mascara stains on Gina's white shirt, Valerie attempted to wipe them off with a Kleenex.

"I'm so sorry about this; I've ruined your shirt!"

Gina stopped her and said, "Don't worry about it."

Gina pointed to Bob and introduced him to Valerie. She politely thanked him for the water and took a long drink. It gave them a moment to get a good picture of her, now that she had gained composure. Valerie Bruster looked to be in her mid thirties. She was a professional looking woman with a friendly face. She wore a pair of tan slacks and a pretty multicolored blouse. She had brown, curly hair and was on the slender side. Gina noted she was married, based on the gorgeous wedding ring on her finger.

"I don't know where to begin!" exclaimed Valerie. Gina prompted her along as Bob took notes.

"Did you have plans with Denise tonight?"

Valerie replied, "Yes, we were supposed to meet for dinner at Pedro's Cantina at 6:00. Her husband, Mark, is out of town on business and we thought it would be nice to get together just the two of us. When she didn't show up by 6:30, I got worried and came right over."

Valerie hesitated and then continued. "Everything looked normal when I pulled up. Denise's car was parked in the driveway. I thought maybe she had gotten off work late and wanted to go home to change. Or maybe she had completely forgotten to meet me. As I rang the doorbell, I noticed the door wasn't closed all the way. I began to get worried because Denise always locked her doors. I stepped inside and yelled her name, but heard nothing. I began to search the house for her and later found her in the bedroom."

Gina asked, "Did you touch anything in the bedroom?"

Valerie nodded before answering, "Yes, I did. I used the phone beside her on the nightstand to call 911. I didn't know what else to do. I had checked for a pulse in her neck and arm, but found none. There was blood everywhere." A tear began to trickle down Valerie's face and her hands began to shake.

Gina gently clasped Valerie's hand and asked, "Did you see anyone in the vicinity of the house when you arrived?"

"No, just some kids riding their bikes down the street. I didn't see anything out of the ordinary until I noticed the front door was ajar."

Gina plodded onward. "Did Denise ever have any enemies or did she ever mention anyone to you that was giving her problems?"

Valerie shrugged her shoulders before replying, "She had some weird clients, but that was nothing new. She never really spoke about any of them in particular. She strived to keep it out of her personal life, especially around Mark. He never wanted her to be a probation officer because he felt it was an unrewarding and dangerous profession."

"Where is Mark now?" asked Gina.

"He had a sales meeting in Denver for McGregor Incorporated, but I don't know exactly where he's staying. He's supposed to be back tomorrow."

With hesitation in her voice, Gina said, "I'm sorry, but I have to ask. Did they have a good marriage?"

"They had problems like all of us, but it was never anything major. A lot of their friction only began when she took this job. Mark wanted to have children and she wanted to wait a few more years."

Bob burst into the conversation. "What about her personal life? Can you think of anyone who would want to harm her?"

Valerie quickly responded, "No, she was a wonderful woman who was well liked."

Gina added, "We'll need you to come down to the station tomorrow to make an official statement. Go home and get some rest. I'll have an officer drive you. You don't need to be driving right now. Will your husband be home?"

"Yes," Valerie answered. Gina introduced her to Officer Brooks and the two quickly left the house.

The search for clues continued at 4804 Rosemont. Forced entry was found at the living room window, at the same place the neighbor had seen a man trying to break in on Friday night. The screen had been cut and the lock jimmied. The intruder most likely climbed through the window and waited for Denise Steidman to come home from work. He then tortured and killed her upstairs. Ralph Faraday thought she had been raped, but would know better upon completion of the autopsy. After the vicious act was done, the intruder apparently just walked out the front door. This was why it was found ajar by Valerie Bruster.

Officers had questioned all of the neighbors on the block, but no one had seen or heard anything out of the ordinary. An elderly woman who lived across the street had seen Steidman arrive home shortly after 5 PM, but never saw anyone else around the house until Bruster arrived.

There were no prints found anywhere. While uniformed officers were logging and bagging all the evidence, Bob and Gina searched for a phone number where the victim's husband was staying in Denver. Bob found it scribbled on the calendar in the kitchen.

He looked at Gina and said, "It's my turn. I'll handle this one."

He took a deep breath and then dialed the number. A man answered, "Embassy Hotel, how can I help you?"

Bob answered, "Please transfer me to Mark Steidman's room."

"Certainly," the man replied. The line rang 5 times before the hotel desk clerk interrupted, "Mr. Steidman is not answering. Would you like to leave a message?"

Bob left his name and phone number with the clerk. He added that it was urgent and Mr. Steidman should return the call as soon as he returned. Bob hung up the phone with a temporary sigh of relief. It was torture to tell someone a loved one had died, let alone been brutally murdered.

"Mark's not at the hotel?" Gina asked as she looked at her watch. It was after midnight.

"No, I left a message for him to call me right away."

They continued to search the house and perimeter for further clues until the early morning hours, but found no additional evidence.

Bob stated, "There's nothing more we can do here tonight, Gina. The uniforms will secure the scene. Let's go home and get a couple hours rest." She nodded in agreement.

There were only a few officers left when they pulled out of the driveway. They sat in silence for a few minutes before Bob asked, "Are you okay, Gina? I know you and Denise were friends."

Gina slowly stated, "We were just getting to know each other better. We had worked joint cases together for several years, but didn't socialize outside of work. She was a very sweet woman who didn't deserve this, not that anyone does. I'm going to nail the sick animal who did this to her!"

Bob announced, "I called the desk sergeant and told him to send an officer over to your apartment."

She asked rather naively, "Why?"

"I'm really worried about you," he replied. "Some psychopath wants you dead. He's already shown us he is capable of taking a life. And for some reason, he wants you to know he's coming for you. It's a game to him; you know that."

"Yes, I do. In my defense, I'm not some ditzy college girl. I plan to catch this animal and beat him at his own perverse game," Gina said calmly.

"Why don't you stay with Lisa and me tonight?" he asked.

"Thanks, Bob, but I'll be fine. I have an officer standing guard. And besides, you and Lisa need some time alone."

She looked away as soon as she said it, knowing she may have slipped up. Bob had not mentioned anything about Lisa's pregnancy. Maybe Lisa didn't get the chance to tell him before he got the call.

"What do you mean we need some time alone?"

Gina paused before replying, "Nothing. I just know it's important for married people to have time together. I don't want to be a third wheel." She stared into his eyes, hoping he would accept her explanation.

He raised his voice. "Damn it, Gina! I'm your partner. I want to help you get through this. I know you're very independent, but you shouldn't be alone with everything that's happened!"

Gina smiled as she said, "I won't be." Bob sat pensively in silence and then a grin formed on his face.

"So you and Ted are getting along well?"

"It's not what you're thinking, at least not yet. He's a nice man who I plan to get to know better."

As Bob stopped the car in front of her apartment complex, he got a serious look on his face. "Gina, promise me that you'll have Ted stay with you tonight and you'll call me if there are any problems."

She kissed his cheek gently and said, "I promise. Thank you for caring about me so much." As she stepped out of the car and walked into the building, she saw Officer Kimble stepping out of the elevator.

He said, "I saw you drive up through the hallway window and thought I'd escort you upstairs." She thanked him and they stepped onto the elevator.

She said, "I'm sorry you got stuck with this assignment again. I'm sure it must be very boring for you."

"It's not that bad. I'm well rested; I just came on at midnight."

The elevator doors opened and they walked down the hallway to her apartment. He tried to reassure her. "I'm sure the guy's long gone by now. But just as a precaution, I need to check your apartment."

With both of their guns drawn, they entered and began to canvas the apartment. They searched everywhere: under her bed, in the closets, on the balcony. All was clear on the home front. A soft breath hissed through her lips as they holstered their weapons.

Officer Kimble left the apartment and resumed his watch in the hallway. She was finally alone and didn't quite know what to do with herself. She was still very shaken by the whole thing and visions of Denise Steidman's mutilated body flashed through her mind. She could put up a strong front for Bob and the others, but she couldn't trick herself. She was terrified of this man and what he planned to do to her. His madness seemed unstoppable and she still had no real clues to his identity. This frustration only worsened her anxiety. She sat still in confusion and then she remembered her promise.

She quickly got up and unlocked her door. Kimble arose from his chair and asked, "Is everything okay?"

"Yes, I'm just going to visit Ted." She knocked at the door across the hall and a moment later, Ted opened the door groggily. He was wearing only a pair of navy blue boxers and had obviously been asleep.

"I know it's really late. I'm sorry to wake you, but I need some company."

He immediately answered, "Sure, come on in."

Ted closed the door behind them and grabbed her hand. "Are you alright, Gina?"

A tear began to trickle down the left side of her face as she softly said, "No." He pulled her weary body against his bare chest and hugged her tightly.

He asked, "Do you want to talk about it?"

She shook her head, "No, I just want to feel safe. Can I stay here tonight?" Ted looked rather stunned. Before he could answer, Gina cut him off. "Wait a minute. Let me be clear about this. As appealing as you look, I'm very vulnerable right now and don't want to do something we would regret later."

Ted smiled and replied, "I'm certain I wouldn't regret making love to you, quite the contrary. But I understand and respect your feelings. Do you want to watch some TV or do you just want to go to bed?"

Gina despondently stated, "I just want to go to bed."

Ted laughed and said, "I've never gotten that response before. Where have you been all my life?"

She smiled in return and he led her to his bedroom. Ted put on a t-shirt while Gina took off her shoes. She then set her weapon down on the nightstand and laid down on the bed. He turned off the lights and joined her in bed.

"Do you need to be up by any certain time?" he asked.

"By 7:00, please." He rolled over and put his arm around her.

"You're safe now," he murmured confidently.

She closed her eyes and desperately tried to forget the image of Denise's butchered body lying on the bed. She felt so fortunate to know someone like Ted at a time like this. The warmth of his body against hers proved to her that she was not alone. She would manage to get through it somehow, just as she had done in the past when tragedy struck. She would not allow herself to be beaten by this murderer or life itself. If anything, her spirit would strengthen because of the difficult tests life had presented her. She would pass with flying colors.

CHAPTER 8

Gina opened her eyes to the annoying beeping of Ted's alarm clock. She expected Ted to shut it off, but she was alone in the bed. She leaned over and turned it off herself. She glanced around the room, while rubbing her eyes. There was still no sign of Ted. She got out of bed and walked slowly into the living room. She then spotted a piece of paper on the coffee table. It read, "Went out for doughnuts. Be back soon."

She decided she would go back to her apartment and take a shower. She picked up her shoes and stuck her gun in the back of her jeans. She opened the door to the hallway and was startled. She immediately dropped her shoes and pulled out her 9 millimeter. The officer was gone and the door to her apartment left partially open! She looked down the hallway, but all was quiet. With her gun drawn, she gently pushed her door wide open with her foot. Her eyes quickly scanned the kitchen and living room. Her attention was captured at her kitchen table. A message was written in ketchup on the table. It read, "It's only a matter of time."

She took a deep breath and carefully made her way down the hallway to her bedroom. She stopped at the corner and hid behind the doorframe. She listened, but heard nothing. She quickly stepped into the bedroom with the shiny glare of her weapon drawn in front of her. No one was there and nothing was out of place. She methodically checked under the bed and in the closets. She stepped into the bathroom and her eyes focused on the shower curtain, which was fully extended. With one quick tug, she pulled the shower curtain back! But only an empty tub lay before her.

She took a small step backward out of relief, but her body was thwarted by something behind her. She spun around, with her weapon aimed. This action prompted a box of Dunkin Doughnuts to be dropped to the floor.

"Shit, Gina! It's only me!" snapped a pale-faced Ted.

She brought down her weapon and screamed, "You don't sneak up on me like that! Are you nuts?"

"I'm sorry, Gina," he stammered. " I just got back and was worried when I didn't find you in my apartment. I thought you and the officer were over here. Where is he anyway?"

Gina brushed past him while saying, "I don't know." She left the apartment and walked carefully down the hallway. She approached the door to the stairwell and tried to push the door open. But it was blocked and would not open more than a few inches. She tried to kick it open, but it didn't budge. She stuck her weapon in the back of her jeans and pushed her right shoulder into the door. It moved some, and she was able to slide through the doorway.

What lay on the other side of the door was Officer Kimble. He was face down and not moving. She felt for a pulse in his neck. Ted yelled from the other side of the door, "What's going on? Is everything okay?" Gina didn't answer, as she was still searching for some signs of life from Officer Kimble. Finally, she felt a pulse. She ordered Ted, "Go call for an ambulance!"

She rolled the officer over, with urgency in her voice. "Officer Kimble, wake up!" He began to moan and reached for his head, which was bleeding behind his right ear. "You're going to be fine," she told him, as she pressed firmly on the wound to control the bleeding.

He mumbled, "What happened?"

She shrugged her shoulders and said, "I was going to ask you the same thing. I came out of Ted's apartment and found you gone and my door open. I checked it out, but no one was there. But he had been there."

Officer Kimble added, "Shortly after Ted left, I heard noises coming from this stairwell. It sounded like someone had fallen down the stairs. I rushed down here to see if anyone was hurt. I remember opening this door and then being hit in the head from behind. I never saw who did it."

Ted's voice came from the other side of the door. "The ambulance is on the way."

She replied, "Good. Could you bring me the phone and a towel?"

With that, Ted's footsteps were heard running down the hall. A moment later, he returned and handed Gina the phone and towel. She pressed the towel against the gash on the officer's head. She then called Bob at home and told him what had happened. He told her he would be right over.

A few minutes later, a siren wailed in the distance. Ted went downstairs to meet them and proceeded to show them the way to Officer Kimble. Gina had helped Kimble move away from the door, thus allowing the paramedics to get through. She got up from her kneeling position on the floor and stepped back to give the paramedics some room.

"What was he hit with?" asked the younger of the two paramedics.

"I don't know," Gina answered. "He didn't see it coming."

They examined the cut and placed him on a stretcher. As she was escorting them down the hallway, the doors of the elevator opened and Bob appeared, along with a couple of uniformed officers.

Bob anxiously asked, "Is everyone okay?"

Gina and Officer Kimble simultaneously answered, "Yes."

She and Bob said good-bye to Kimble, as he was wheeled onto the elevator. This left Gina, Bob, Ted, and two uniformed officers standing in the hallway. In addition, several residents came out to see what was going on.

She pulled Bob aside and said, "Come look what he left for me." They entered her apartment and Bob stared at the message left on her kitchen table. The bottle of ketchup which was used to write the message, lay innocently on the floor under the table.

Bob turned to the other two officers and stated, "Guys, we need to get some pictures of this."

They headed for their patrol cars to get the proper equipment. Bob walked through the apartment, surveying the situation.

He stopped at the bathroom and asked, "Why is there a box of doughnuts on the floor?"

Ted chuckled, "Because your partner scared the shit out of me." Bob looked at Gina with bewilderment.

Gina explained what had happened. "I stayed at Ted's last night. When I woke up this morning, he had gone to get doughnuts. I decided to go back to my apartment and take a shower. When I opened the door, I saw Officer Kimble was gone and my door was ajar. I went through the apartment and found no one, just the message on the table. Ted came up on me from behind and I turned around with my gun pointed at him, causing him to drop the doughnuts. I then looked for Officer Kimble and found him in the stairwell unconscious."

"What time did all this happen?" Bob inquired.

Gina answered, "I can tell you almost exactly. The alarm went off at 7 AM and I left Ted's apartment within a couple minutes." Bob's attention then turned to Ted.

"At what time did you leave for doughnuts and was the officer in the hallway when you left?"

Ted thought about it for a moment and then informed, "I'm not exactly sure when I left, but the officer was still there." Bob's voice became rather stern.

"Look, man, this is important. When would you estimate leaving?"

Gina butted in, "Bob, what's going on? You have no reason to be rude to Ted." Before Bob could respond, Ted answered the original question.

"I would guess it was about 6:30 or a little later. I woke up at about 6:20 and saw Gina was still sleeping peacefully. I didn't want to wake her, so I got dressed in the bathroom and then left to get doughnuts."

Gina glared at Bob and then Ted said, "I'm sorry, Gina. I have to leave for work." He left abruptly, as the two uniformed officers entered the apartment. The argument immediately ensued.

"Bob, I can't believe you treated him that way!"

"I just asked the man a question." The two officers stared at them, prompting them to take their discussion to the bedroom.

Bob began, "You have my utmost respect. But I don't think you're thinking clearly right now. And with everything that's been happening, I can certainly understand that. Who you choose to share your bed with, is your business. I just didn't think Ted was taking this seriously. I care about you and don't want to see you harmed in any way. Is that wrong?"

Gina sighed heavily. "Of course, that's not wrong. Maybe I'm just on the defensive when it comes to Ted, because I'm really starting to like him. I don't think he intended to be evasive. He was just flustered at having a gun pointed at his chest. You forget the average person doesn't experience the things we do."

Bob nodded in agreement, as Gina piped in. "Oh, and let's set something else straight. Not that it's any of your concern, but I didn't sleep with Ted last night. Yes, in the strictly literal sense, I did. But it was nothing more than that. I have to admit this whole thing is really getting to me."

He answered, "I know what you mean. Lisa and I were enjoying a nice, romantic dinner last night when I got the call about the attack. It's amazing how quickly life can turn on you. One minute, you're spending a wonderful evening with your wife and the next, you're looking at a body torn to shreds! I'm really worried about you, Gina. Whoever this guy is, he's not going to just go away. You know that, don't you?"

"Yes, I know. I'm sorry I snapped at you."

"Don't worry about it."

They then walked to the kitchen, where flash photography lit up the room. One officer was taking pictures, while the other was dusting for latent fingerprints on the refrigerator door. The phone began to ring and Gina picked it up. It was Chief Buchanon. He wanted Gina and Bob to come to the office right away to discuss the case. They quickly left her apartment to the other officers.

As they exited the building, Bob suggested taking his car. They hopped in and continued to talk about the case on the way to the station. He said, "I should go to the county jail today and talk to Dwayne Timbers. He could have ordered a hit on you and Steidman from lockup."

Gina insisted, "I want to go, too. I know I shouldn't talk to him directly because I'm too involved. But you could interview him in an interrogation room with tinted glass. I could watch and he wouldn't even know I was there. I just want to be a part of it, Bob. Don't shut me out!"

He finally conceded, "Okay, you can come."

Gina added, "I still haven't given up on John Utik, either."

Bob gruffly stated, "Forget you ever heard that man's name, Gina. The Chief would have your ass if he knew you were even thinking about him! Besides, didn't you get chewed out enough by Judge Slocum in his chambers? I could hear him yelling through the walls of the courthouse. Even when he came back into the courtroom, he couldn't hide his anger. It was written all over his face."

"It was worth it because I felt I was doing the right thing."

He changed the subject. "I'm just glad you didn't stay in your apartment last night. It scares me to think about what could have happened. From now on, I'm staying with you or I'm taking you to a safehouse. I'm also going to request more officers be assigned to guard you."

Gina responded quickly. "Now is not the time for you to be away from Lisa."

He questioned, "What do you mean by that?" Gina knew she had slipped and tried to recover, as it was apparent Bob still didn't know that Lisa was pregnant.

"I just meant now would be the time to correct things. You told me she had been distant towards you lately. So, now would be the time she needs you the most. Right?"

"I guess you're right, Gina. But you're my partner and I intend to keep you safe."

As they pulled up to the station, she inquired, "Have you spoken with Denise Steidman's husband, Mark?"

"No, he hasn't returned my call. I find that very strange, don't you?"

"Certainly," she responded. They got out of the car and walked to the detective division, where they were immediately greeted by Chief Buchanon.

"In my office, now!" yelled the Chief. They followed him inside and sat down before him. The Chief continued, "Perry, I'm glad you're alright and Kimble will be fine. But what the hell kind of leads have we got? The mayor has already called me this morning, demanding we find this killer now."

Bob informed, "We plan to go talk to Dwayne Timbers in the county jail today to see if we can get anything out of him."

Chief Buchanon interrupted, "I'm afraid that won't be possible. Timbers was killed in jail last night. He and another inmate got into a fight and he was strangled." Gina and Bob looked at each other in total disbelief.

"Was he your only suspect?" demanded the Chief.

Gina looked at Bob and Bob knew she was thinking of John Utik. He had used a serrated hunting knife in the attack on Shirley Jenson. Everyone knew he did it. Then there were other attacks involving the same type of knife. Plus, he had threatened Gina countless times. Yet, Bob still didn't think Utik was the culprit. Utik was not smart enough. Before Gina could bring up Utik to the Chief, Bob began to speak.

"Chief, we're doing everything we can. I'm personally planning to stay with Gina tonight, whether it be at her apartment or a safehouse."

"I'm not going to a safehouse," Gina insisted. "I want this over with, and that would only delay it. Let's just set a trap for him at my place. We could have a uniformed officer standing guard for part of the evening. Then the officer could pretend to get an emergency call elsewhere and peel out of the lot with sirens blaring. We would have a few undercover officers around outside, but he would think I'm alone."

"That's too risky," Bob stated firmly.

"What are our other options?" Gina implored. "This guy isn't going to stop and you know it. If he can't get to me, he just goes to some other woman. Look at Denise Steidman. He was interrupted in his attack on me on Thursday night. Then on Friday night, a man is seen lurking outside Denise's house. He's interrupted by Denise's husband, Mark. The Steidman's were out of town Saturday night, so he watches me, instead. He sent me those flowers at Christine's just to let me know he's still out there waiting. The Steidman's come back Sunday night. He must have watched and waited until Mark went out of town on Monday. He kills Denise and comes to my apartment the next morning."

"What's your point, Perry?" urged the Chief.

She answered, "This guy is coming apart at the seams. He now knows he is capable of killing. If you take me to a safehouse or surround me with uniforms, it may protect me, but only hurt someone else. He will simply pick another hapless victim to satisfy his urges. And I'm not going to stand for it! Denise's death was more than enough! Let's put an end to it now! It's me he wants and it's me, he'll get!"

Chief Buchanon could be crude at times, and judging by the look on his face, this was one of those times. He smiled while saying, "Perry, sometimes I have to remind myself you're a female. You've got more balls than some of the men in this outfit!" Bob intervened.

"With all due respect, sir, I fail to find the humor in this. We would really be placing Gina in danger by taking the uniforms away. I don't like it!"

The Chief leaned back in his chair and told Bob, "Too bad, Wilson. We need an arrest on this case and we need it soon. From now on, I want surveillance on Perry whenever she's not at work. I don't think this guy will try anything during the workday; it's not his method of operation. If she's with you, we don't need a second car. But after 5 PM, I'm assigning Logan and Rogers to her also. It's up to Perry if she wants any of you in her apartment with her."

Gina suggested, "I could wear a wire to ease your mind, Bob. If we had someone in the apartment with me, we would run the risk of this guy seeing them go into the apartment building. I'm sure he knows all your faces by now. Just give me a chance to bring this guy out in the open."

Bob nervously bit his fingernails as Chief Buchanon stated, "Then it's all settled. Perry, come in this afternoon to get wired up."

"Yes, sir," she replied.

As Gina and Bob left the Chief's office, Bob's cell phone rang. He glanced down at the number on the screen, but didn't recognize it.

"Maybe it's Mark Steidman," he said, as he answered, "Detective Wilson."

A man's voice replied, "This is Mark Steidman. I had a message at the hotel in Denver to call you. I was out late last night with clients. I didn't get the message until I was on my way out to the airport this morning."

Bob quickly asked, "Where are you calling from?"

"I'm in town at the airport. I didn't get a chance to call before I left Denver. What's going on?"

Bob calmly stated, "I need you to come down to the station right away. I'll tell you all about it then."

Mark became somewhat irritated and said, "Look, just tell me what's going on and we can set up an appointment. I don't have time for this right now. I'm on my way home to drop things off and then I have a sales meeting downtown."

Bob's voice was unwavering, "This isn't something we should talk about over the phone. Just come on in, Mr. Steidman. I will answer all your questions then." Steidman finally agreed and Bob hung up the phone.

Gina volunteered, "I'll help you tell him." Bob stared blankly at the wall and nodded his head in agreement.

Although only half an hour had passed, the time spent waiting for Mark Steidman to arrive seemed like an eternity. Finally, they saw him get off the elevator and ask for Detective Wilson. Gina and Bob arose from their desks and walked towards Steidman, who looked both confused and irritated. After everyone was introduced and hands were shaken, Bob led them into an interview room.

Steidman began, "Now, what's so damn important?" With Gina and Bob sitting on one side of the table and Steidman on the other, Bob began to tell him what had happened.

"Mr. Steidman, I'm afraid I have some very bad news. There is no easy way to say it, so I'll just come out with it. Your wife, Denise, was killed last night."

Before Bob could continue, Steidman broke in. "Killed? How? What happened?"

"Someone broke into your house and killed her. I'm truly sorry, Mr. Steidman." In complete shock, Steidman shook his head in utter disbelief.

"There must be some mistake. It can't be true. She was fine yesterday. I called her in the afternoon at work. She was planning to have dinner with her friend, Valerie."

Bob added, "Yes, she was planning to meet Mrs. Bruster, but she didn't make it to the restaurant. Mrs. Bruster found her in your home. It was too late."

Steidman buried his face in his hands and began to sob. He then laid his head down on the table and hit the table with his fist. Bob looked at Gina, as a tear began to trickle down the right side of her face. She stood up, walked around the table, and sat down in the chair beside Steidman. She put her arm around his heaving shoulders and said, "My heart goes out to you, Mark. I knew Denise and she was a wonderful woman who didn't deserve this."

He looked up at Gina and could see the sincerity in her teary eyes. He immediately turned to her and they embraced. He continued to cry while stammering, "I love her so much! I can't imagine life without her!" His sobs continued as he sniveled against Gina's chest. Bob sat quietly across the table, not quite knowing what to say. What could be said? This man's wife was not only gone, but was butchered in their own bed.

After a few moments, Mark Steidman sat up in his chair and desperately tried to compose himself. Gina handed him a tissue, which he accepted. He then turned to Gina and asked, "Exactly how was she killed? I need to know."

Gina shook her head and answered, "Now is not really the best time for that; you have enough to deal with."

"I'm begging you! If you cared at all for my wife, you'll tell me. Don't I have a right to know?"

She thought for a moment and then agreed. "Of course, you have a right to know. We were just trying to spare you some of the agonizing details. Denise was stabbed to death in your bedroom." Gina hoped he would leave it at that for now, but he persisted.

"Was she raped?" he asked sorrowfully.

Bob intervened by saying, "It's uncertain yet. It's an ongoing investigation. We will keep you informed as information develops."

Steidman asked angrily, "Have you caught the guy?"

"Not yet," Gina quickly responded. "But we will do everything in our power to see that happen."

"Do you know of anyone who would want to harm your wife?" Bob inquired.

"No, other than some of her crazy clients," Steidman retorted. "I warned her about taking that job. Now look what's happened!"

Gina continued, "Did she ever mention any in particular that had given her problems?" The response was negative.

Bob stated, "I need you to make out a list of the clients you were with last night in Denver."

"Am I a suspect?" Steidman asked.

Bob replied, "It's standard procedure in a case like this to rule people out. If you could just write down their names and phone numbers, if you have them." Steidman pulled out a pocket organizer from his jacket and began searching for the names. Gina handed him a piece of paper and he began writing the information down.

He said, "There were six of us who went out for drinks, but I don't have phone numbers for two of them."

Bob stated, "That's not a problem." Steidman completed the list and slid it across the table to Bob.

Bob informed him the house was cordoned off as a crime scene and he would probably want to stay at a hotel or with relatives for now. Gina offered him a ride to his parents' house, stating he shouldn't be driving right now. He graciously declined and said he would be alright. Gina and Bob escorted him to the elevator and told him they would speak with him tomorrow. Red eyed, his head low, he stepped into the elevator and pushed the button for the first floor. The doors closed before him, almost as an analogy to his existence. Part of his life had been ripped apart, leaving a grief-stricken man standing in an empty cavern of himself.

CHAPTER 9

Gina and Bob divided the names on Mark Steidman's list of clients and began making phone calls to each of them. His alibi checked out. They all said they went out for drinks and didn't leave the bar until after 1 AM. Gina and Bob then left the station and had a light lunch before heading for the morgue to speak with the coroner, Ralph Faraday. As they walked into the building, Bob stopped.

"Look, Gina, you don't have to go in the room and see the body again. I know you and Denise were friends and I think it would be too much for you to take. I could fill you in on the results."

Not to his surprise, she firmly stated, "I got through it last night. I'm going to give it a try. If it's too much, I'll leave. But, maybe it would be best if you questioned Faraday."

"No problem, Gina."

Bob knocked on the door of the autopsy room and Faraday appeared. He nonchalantly said, "Hi, guys. Come on in. She's right over here."

Gina took a deep breath and followed the two men to the sheet-covered table near the window. As he pulled back the sheet, Gina tried to keep her feelings intact. She would never fathom how Faraday could do this for a living and seem so disconnected from the loss of human life. But he definitely had it mastered.

Faraday began to share his findings. "This is a piece of work. The person who did this is definitely out of control. But when he begins the attack, he is fully in control. Look at these wounds." He pointed to her abdomen and lower chest area, which were literally ripped apart from side to side. He continued, "The first 7 or 8 slicings are superficial and in an organized pattern from left to right. He also made shallow cuts to her breasts, ones which he knew would not be fatal. May I suggest he wants her to know what's coming before he kills her? After those cuts, he loses his cool and just makes random incisions. I counted a total of 18 cuts in her abdomen and pelvic region. The knife he used had jagged edges. It looked like some type of hunting knife, about 6-7 inches long."

Faraday then pointed to the markings in her upper chest and said to Gina, "Looks like you have an admirer. By the way, this was done post-mortem. She was killed between 5 PM and 6 PM. That message was carved in her chest right after she died from the loss of blood and severe trauma to the abdominal aorta.

Gina took a step backward and leaned against the window. She stared at the body, but remained silent.

Bob asked, "Was she sexually assaulted?"

Faraday confirmed, "Yes. However, I found no semen. I combed for hair samples, but found none, either. The man who did this was very careful."

Gina turned away and stared pensively out the window. Was this to be her fate? Would she one day be lying on that very table with Faraday scrutinizing every inch of her body's remains? She began to feel light-headed and her stomach ached. She couldn't bear another moment in the room.

She ran out and headed for the women's restroom down the hall. She locked herself in a stall and began vomiting in the toilet. She knelt down on the floor for a few minutes and hoped her stomach had no more left to offer.

A woman in a nearby stall asked, "Are you okay?"

Gina responded, "I'm fine, thanks." Gina had hung around men long enough to know however bad things were, you always said you were fine.

As she heard the woman's heels exiting the bathroom, the woman shrieked. "You don't belong in here! This is a ladies' room! Can't you read?" Gina snickered, as she realized the woman was yelling at Bob.

He told the woman, "I'm a cop, ma'am. My partner's in there." She heard the door swing closed and heavy footsteps neared her.

Just on the other side of the stall door, Bob stood. "Gina, come out. Are you okay?"

She jokingly replied, "I'm just great. I just had to cough up a lung or two, as well as a ham and Swiss sandwich."

Bob laughed and said, "You didn't have to be that detailed." Gina picked herself up off the floor and opened the stall door. He took a step backward, to let her through. She walked to the sink and washed her face with cool water.

"I guess you were right about me going in there," she said, as she looked at him in the mirror.

"Frankly, Faraday's account of that poor woman was starting to get to me, too," he admitted.

She grabbed a paper towel from the dispenser behind him and said, "Let's get out of here before some old lady beats you with her purse." He chuckled and followed her out of the restroom. They left the building and got into their car.

"Did Faraday say anything important after I left?" questioned Gina.

"Yes, he said the man who did this is right handed based on the angle of the slashings. He couldn't approximate the man's height because all of the slashings occurred while she was lying on the bed. Let me think, was there anything else? Oh yeah, she was alive when he raped her."

Gina wanted to confide to Bob how she was truly feeling. She was scared beyond belief. But if he knew, he would never go along with their plans tonight. He would want every officer in the department protecting her. So for now, she had to keep her emotions hidden as best as possible around him. She had to catch this man any way she could. She would deal with the emotional repercussions later.

As they pulled out of the morgue parking lot, she looked at her watch; it was 1:30 PM. She suggested they split up to get more done. She could go to the probation office and talk with Denise Steidman's co-workers, while Bob went back to the neighborhood to see if anyone else had seen or heard anything. He agreed and dropped her off at the station, where she checked out an unmarked gray Chevy from the police garage.

She drove to the probation office and walked inside, with her notebook in hand. Everyone already knew what had happened to Denise and the mood there was very somber. Many were still in shock and others cried openly. Gina spoke to Denise's supervisor and several co-workers. They all echoed the same thoughts. They couldn't believe Denise was dead and had no idea who would have done such a thing. She had awful clients, just like the rest, but they knew of none who had threatened or harassed her openly. Everyone in the office liked and respected Denise. Gina also learned Denise had left the office on Monday afternoon at about 4:30 PM. She had told one co-worker she was going home to change, before having dinner with a girlfriend.

Gina went through Denise's desk, hoping to find some clues, but found nothing unusual. She thanked them all for their help and expressed her condolences. She left the probation office with a frown on her face and a lump in her throat. Her sadness turned to anger, and then to determination. She would catch this animal, no matter what! She drove to the station and slowly walked into the building. She was dazed, as she made her way upstairs to the detective division.

She arrived at her desk to find a message that Derick had called and wanted to talk to her. He asked that she call him back. She pitched the message in the trash. Logan and Rogers came over to her desk and Rogers said, "I guess we've got you tonight."

She smiled and answered, "Looks like it."

Logan asked, "What kind of monitoring device are you planning to use?"

She immediately answered, "I want to use a body wire with a recorder and transmitter. If this guy should come tonight, I want to get him on tape. I'm sure he's aching to tell me all the horrific things he's done. In his mind, he has nothing to lose by telling me because he will kill me, anyway."

Logan restated, "So you want us to wait even after we hear him attack you? That's insane!"

Gina coaxed, "Come on, guys. Think about it. If you bust down the door immediately, what will happen in the courts? Maybe he'll do time for breaking and entering? Or if we're lucky, assault? That's not enough. I want him connected to the other rapes and Steidman homicide. Give me some time to talk to him."

With a concerned look on his face, Logan responded. "Perry, this man's not going to break into your apartment for mere conversation. He wants to hurt you in the worst ways."

"I understand what you're saying," Gina agreed. "Believe me, I do. But I feel like I'm getting to know this guy. He'll want to brag about the things he's done and what he plans to do to me. That's half of his enjoyment. He gets off on it. The fear he creates, gives him power and control, which he so desperately wants to show."

She proceeded to brief them on the results of Denise Steidman's autopsy. She also told them about the break-in at her apartment that morning. Unfortunately, the officers had found no fingerprints. They further discussed how they would handle the surveillance at her apartment. They would have a van parked nearby to monitor the electronic surveillance. Bob would be in the area in his car. Uniforms in the area would be notified of the stakeout and be ready to roll if needed.

Chief Buchanon was apprised of the plans and simply stated, "Call me right away if anything goes down." As he walked away, he turned to Gina and informed her, "Officer Knight will be here any moment to help you with the body wire. She just got off patrol. I've also assigned her to help at your place tonight in plainclothes." He then continued on his way to his office and sat down at his desk.

Gina called the hospital to check on Officer Kimble. She learned he was doing fine, but they wanted to keep him overnight for observation. She shared the news with Logan and Rogers, as Officer Knight stepped off the elevator and made her way towards Gina's desk. Gina stood up, extended her right hand, and said, "Good to see you, Pam. How have you been?"

The two women shook hands as Pam replied, "I've been doing alright, Gina. I'm sorry things are like this for you, though."

Gina said, "It's all going to end soon. I'm glad you're working on it with us."

"Me, too," Pam added. "Now let's go get you hooked up to all this." She looked downward at the briefcase she was carrying. Gina took off her jacket and placed it on the back of her chair. She and Pam then headed for the women's restroom on the same floor.

As they walked away, someone yelled in a lewd tone, "If you two ladies need any help, I'm at your service."

Chief Buchanon heard the comment and barked, "Everything is to be done by the book, gentlemen! We don't need any more harassment charges around here!"

He was referring to a lawsuit filed by another female officer in the department, who alleged sexual harassment and discrimination because she was passed over for promotion to detective. Gina was, in fact, the only female detective in the department.

Pam Knight was a competent officer whom everyone assumed would make detective within the next year or so. She was in her late twenties, about 5'8", with a slender build. She had blonde hair, which frequently prompted all the dumb blonde jokes from the guys. But she handled it quite well and Gina respected her for it. Gina had learned with time, not to sweat the small stuff, and to focus on the bigger issues at hand. If comments and jokes got out of hand, then she definitely stood up for herself. But most of the time, they were innocent enough.

Pam set the metal briefcase down on the couch in the restroom, opened it up, and began removing the monitoring devices. Meanwhile, Gina took off her shirt and threw it on the couch. Pam then picked up the recording unit and taped it to Gina's lower back. Next, Pam ran the wires up her back and over her shoulders. The microphone and transmitter were taped to the front of her chest.

Pam asked, "Aren't we going to be recording in the van also?"

"Yes, but I want to have both just in case something goes wrong or I get out of range. This one only transmits about 100 yards."

Pam noticed that Gina's right shoulder was bruised and asked what had happened. Gina told her all about what had happened that morning, including how she had to push the stairwell door open with her shoulder. Gina guessed that was how it had been bruised.

In the midst of their discussion, the restroom door burst open and in hurried Bob. "Gina, what's going on? The guys told me you want us to wait to come in until you have a chance to talk to him?"

Gina retorted, "Bob, we're kind of busy right now. Can't we talk about this outside in a minute?"

Pam agreed, "Really, Bob, you shouldn't be in here."

Bob quickly turned his back to them, as if he just realized he was standing in the middle of the ladies' restroom and his partner was half dressed. While facing the opposite direction, he apologized for barging in. Then he asked in a serious manner, "Since when have you guys had a couch in the bathroom? We've never had a couch in the men's room."

Gina and Pam laughed before Gina replied, "It's always been here, Bob." With that, he exited the restroom.

"That's some partner you've got, Gina," replied Pam.

Gina grinned and nodded in agreement. "Yes, he is."

Pam finished putting the equipment on Gina and asked, "How does that feel?"

"Fine," Gina responded, "but let's try it out now." They went on to test it for sound quality and volume. Everything was fine. They were ready to go.

Pam reminded her, "Don't say or do anything tonight you don't want the guys to hear." Gina smiled in acknowledgment and then got dressed.

The two gathered the remainder of the equipment and left the restroom. Bob was eagerly waiting at the door.

"Gina, you can't go through with this. I don't like it."

"I'm sorry, Bob. But I already have the Chief's approval. Let's just work together and catch this guy, okay?" He shrugged his shoulders in defeat and nodded.

She changed the subject by asking, "So, what did you find out in the Steidman neighborhood?"

"Nothing new from what the officers learned last night," Bob informed. "An elderly woman across the street saw Denise come home shortly before 5 PM, but didn't see anyone after that until Valerie Bruster arrived. None of the kids in the neighborhood saw or heard anything, either. Mary Thompson, the next door neighbor you and

Logan interviewed on Saturday, wasn't home between 5 and 7 PM last night, so she didn't know anything. But she did recall seeing Denise's car in the driveway when she left."

Gina then told Bob the details of her interviews at the probation office. He added, "I made another stop, also. There's a bar down on 8th Street where a lot of Timbers' friends hang out. I just wanted to ask around to see if he had anything to do with all of this."

Bob paused for a moment, forcing Gina to ask, "Yeah, so what happened?"

He answered in a disheartened tone, "I talked to several of Dwayne Timbers' friends. His cousin even stopped in while I was there. None of them claimed to know anything about him ordering any hits. Naturally, I was vague with them about the details. I'm surprised to be saying this, but I don't think Timbers was connected to your attack or the others. Of course, we won't truly know until there is another attack with the same m.o."

Gina was astounded. "Does that mean you think John Utik is involved now?"

Bob quickly silenced her, "Gina, don't even say his name around here. If the Chief heard you, who knows what he would do? And to answer your question, no! I'm still not sold on the idea Utik is our man. I just said I had doubts Timbers was involved."

With a regretful look on her face, she said, "I'm sorry you have to be away from Lisa tonight. Let's just hope this guy shows up, so we can get on with our lives."

Bob responded with sincerity, "Lisa is an understanding woman. You need me more than she does right now." He still didn't know of the pregnancy and Gina was not going to be the one to tell him.

At precisely 5 PM, the entourage of detectives left the station. Bob drove Gina home, since he had picked her up that morning. On the way to her apartment, she turned on her microphone and recorder. The guys following in the van reported back to Bob by hand-held radios. Everything was in proper working condition. As Bob pulled up to her building, he looked over at Gina.

"We'll be right outside, if you need us. What code word do you want to use to tell us it's time to come in?"

"I don't want it to be obvious to this guy there's backup on the way. I don't want him to get out of the apartment. When I tell him I don't want to hear any more of it, it's time for all of you to come in. I don't think it will tip him off."

Bob wished her luck as she exited the car. He then pulled out of the parking lot and drove a couple of miles away before turning back. He wanted to see if anyone was following him and also look for any suspicious vehicles parked nearby. He saw nothing out of the ordinary. He drove past the surveillance van that was parked about a half block away from the apartment building. Inside the van, Detectives Logan, Rogers, and Knight took their positions and waited patiently. Bob drove a block further and parked. He felt very uneasy about the whole situation and a knot developed in his stomach.

Meanwhile, Gina unlocked the door to her apartment and stepped inside. She quickly locked the door behind her. The sound of the locks was transmitted from the apartment to the van outside. She searched the entire apartment before reporting to her comrades, "All clear." She then sat down in the living room and kicked off her shoes. She glanced over at the answering machine and was surprised to find no messages. She hoped Derick would finally realize it was over and leave her alone.

The apartment seemed too quiet, so she turned the television on and watched a comedy sitcom. Her thoughts quickly turned to the surveillance when she heard the uniformed officer get the fake emergency call over his hand-held radio. She then heard him walk down the hallway and a moment later, heard his car siren blaring out of the parking lot. She realized at any moment, the mystery man could appear at her apartment. True, she had backup outside, but unless the guy was John Utik, they wouldn't recognize the man walking into the building. It was a busy apartment complex and people came and went at all hours of the night. She knew the task at hand ultimately fell on her shoulders. Could she handle the pressure? She earnestly tried to focus on the positive side. The sooner this man showed up, the sooner it would all be behind her.

She got up and walked down the hallway to the bathroom. As she unzipped her jeans and prepared to sit down on the toilet, she thankfully remembered she was wired. She turned the water on full blast at the bathroom sink to mask the sounds. After all, who needed a recorded tape of themselves urinating? She recalled a time when she was monitoring a wire in the surveillance van. After hearing the sounds she had heard from a men's restroom, she wished the detective had turned the transmitter off. But she realized that would have only caused alarm on their part, thinking something had gone awry. They also may have missed something important.

She proceeded to wash her hands and on her path back to the living room, was startled by someone knocking on her door. Her heart pounded as a reflex, but her mind remained logical and doubted this man would simply knock at her door. She hurried to the peephole and found Ted standing there. While unlocking the door, she whispered, "It's just my neighbor, Ted." She didn't want everyone listening to get overly excited.

She opened the door and said, "Hi, Ted. How was your day?"

"Fine. I was just worried about you. We need to talk, Gina."

"About what?" she inquired.

"About us. But I'd rather not talk about it out here. May I come in?"

Gina squirmed, realizing everything being said was being monitored. "Actually, Ted, this isn't the best time. It has nothing to do with you. I just need to be alone right now. Can we get together another time?" He seemed flabbergasted.

"Are you sure everything is alright?"

"Yes, I'm sure. Thanks for stopping by."

He turned away despondently and went into his apartment. She glanced down the hallway, but all was quiet. She went back into her apartment and quickly locked the door behind her.

The elusive one sat in deep contemplation. His actions last night had left him rejuvenated. He felt reborn and saw purpose to his life. Yet, he was uncertain how he wanted to handle Detective Perry. Should he make a game of it by stringing her along and eventually driving her mad? Or should he simply rid the world of her meager existence? She had been the most fun thus far, and in an odd way, he might miss her. Either way, she would learn to fear him intensely and respect his power, just as all women should. He relished the day he would have her beside him, for as long as he wished. The simple touch of his hand on her body would bring him such euphoria. He fantasized about how she would scream and plead for her quick death, just as Denise Steidman had done. He never imagined the sound of a woman screaming could be so delightful. But it was, and he basked for a moment remembering previous victims. He then returned his attention to Detective Perry and sat still in the darkness.

CHAPTER 10

Gina watched some more television and began getting hungry. She arose and headed to the kitchen when the phone rang. Her body flinched at the sound. She answered, "Hello." There was no reply, so she again said, "Hello?"

She then heard a woman crying softly and the voice spoke. "Gina, I need to talk to you. Please come over."

Gina responded, "Christine? What's wrong?"

Amidst sniffles and sobs, Christine persisted, "I need to see you right away. It's important." Gina didn't know what to say.

She told Christine, "You know I would be right there if I could. Why won't you tell me what's going on?"

"He hit me, Gina," was the response.

Gina swiftly asked, "Who hit you and is he still there?"

Christine began crying again while mumbling, "Stan hit me. I can't believe what he's done to me."

Gina continued questioning, "Have you called the police?"

"No, he already left. I just want to talk to you, Gina, not the police."

Gina abruptly told her, "I'm on my way."

She hung up the phone and began talking to the other detectives via the microphone. "Look guys, I'm truly sorry, but I have to go see if she's okay. You can all follow me to Christine's. We don't have to stop the surveillance. I need to get going."

As she grabbed her purse and left her apartment, Logan relayed the information to Bob by radio. Gina raced to her car and drove to Christine's, with the surveillance vehicles following behind, careful not to get too close in case anyone else was following her.

She arrived at Christine's apartment complex and hurried into the building. As she rode up in the elevator, she informed, "Okay, guys, I'm going to apartment 412." The elevator doors slowly opened and she walked down the hallway to the last door on the left. She knocked on the door loudly and impatiently waited for Christine to answer. Christine looked through the peephole and unlocked the door. As soon as the door opened, Gina's anger towards Stan escalated to new heights. There stood Christine in a white bathrobe. Her face had been badly beaten. Her left eye was partially closed and a bruise covered her eyelid. Her mouth was swollen and there was a cut on the right side of her face, which continued to bleed.

Gina immediately hugged her and closed the door behind them. Gina walked her into the living room and sat her down on the couch. Christine sat still, not uttering a word. Gina noticed a bloodstained towel on the coffee table, apparently the one Christine had held against the cut on her face. Gina got up, got another towel from the bathroom, and knelt down in front of Christine. She began wiping the cut on Christine's face while asking, "Are you ready to tell me about it?"

Christine looked down and said solemnly, "I'm so embarrassed. If I hadn't let him in, none of this would have happened."

Gina jumped on that statement. "Wait just a minute! This is not your fault! Stan did this to you!" Christine began crying and fell forward, almost knocking Gina off balance as she knelt on the floor. Gina gently pushed her backward and sat beside her on the couch. Gina then wrapped her arms around Christine's crestfallen body. As they embraced, Christine felt the weapon stuck in the waist in the back of Gina's jeans. Before Christine could question her about it, Gina explained the situation.

"We're doing a surveillance tonight. I'm wearing a wire and there are other detectives stationed outside. A woman was murdered last night. I believe the same man who attacked me last week did it." Gina didn't go into the specifics of the case; she wanted to find out exactly what had happened between Stan and Christine.

Gina then stated, "I'm sorry everyone, but I'm turning the wire off just for a few minutes. This is a private conversation that doesn't need to be recorded." Christine simply watched as Gina raised the back of her shirt, fumbled around with the buttons, and turned the recorder off. As Gina and Christine talked openly, her four comrades outside grew increasingly concerned and uneasy.

"Tell me what happened," said Gina in a sympathetic tone. Christine began to tell her story.

"Stan called me this afternoon at work. He wanted to get together tonight and work everything out. He insisted you lied to me about his advances. I told him it was over and I didn't want to see him again. He was outraged and blamed it all on you. He hung up the phone in a rage. I came straight home after work. After dinner, I took a shower. While I was drying off, I heard a knock at the door. I grabbed my bathrobe and put it on as I was walking to the door. I looked through the peephole and saw it was Stan. Gina, I know I shouldn't have let him in, but he didn't seem violent or anything close to it."

Gina again added, "It's not your fault. There is no particular look that men like him have; they come in all shapes and sizes. I've seen many wife and girlfriend beaters who looked like the boy next door. How could you have known? Let's move on. What happened once you let him in here?"

Christine hesitated and then answered, "He was fine at first. He said he just wanted to talk and clear the air. He wanted us to put the 'misunderstanding' regarding you, behind us. I laughed when he called the whole thing a misunderstanding. He got really mad and his demeanor quickly changed. He called you a bitch and said it was a shame I would believe a bitch over the man I loved. I told him I didn't appreciate him bad-mouthing you and it was best he leave. He told me he would leave when he was damn well ready and he wasn't. When I began walking to the door to show him out, he grabbed my arm and pushed me against the wall. He got right in my face and told me it wasn't over between us until he said it was over. Then he punched me in the left eye. I tried to cover my face, but he held my hands above me against the wall. With one hand he controlled my hands, and with his other hand, he hit me in the side of the face. He was wearing a ring, which made this cut." Christine pointed to the gash on the right side of her face, which she had covered by a towel.

Gina continued, "What happened next?"

"I fell to the floor and grabbed my face in pain. As I was bent over, he kicked me in the stomach twice, knocking the wind out of me. Then he left."

Gina looked deeply into Christine's eyes and asked, "Are there any details you're leaving out?"

Christine shook her head and said meekly, "No."

With determination in her voice, Gina inquired further. "Why is there a bite mark on your chest?" Christine quickly looked downward at her upper chest, where her bathrobe parted, and saw the bite mark.

Christine pulled the bathrobe together to cover it and explained, "He did it when he had me pinned against the wall."

"Did it go any further?"

Christine became teary eyed before responding, "No."

Gina gently hugged her and said firmly, "We have to get you to the hospital and have all this checked out. You also need to file a police report and ..."

Christine interrupted her mid-sentence, "I don't want to do any of those things."

Gina's eyes dilated. "You must be kidding. You have injuries that need medical attention and he needs to be arrested. You can't let him get away with this." Christine started to get up from the couch, but quickly sat back down and clutched her right side.

"That's it! We're going to the hospital right now!" exclaimed Gina.

"It's not that bad, really, Gina," pleaded Christine.

"Then move your hand away," demanded Gina. Christine complied and Gina tenderly touched Christine's right side. Christine flinched back in obvious pain.

Gina stated, "You probably have a fractured rib from him kicking you in the stomach. I barely touched it, and that was through a thick bathrobe. You need medical attention."

Gina arose from the couch and extended her hand to Christine. "Come on, you need to put some clothes on." Christine grabbed Gina's hand and they slowly walked to the bedroom.

Christine carefully sat down on the bed, still holding her right side. "I'm still not sure I want to do this, Gina."

As Gina went to the closet to get some clothes, she replied, "Well, I'm positive."

Gina handed her a pair of jeans and shirt before heading to the dresser to look for a bra and underwear, which she found and placed on Christine's lap. "Come on, get dressed. I need to turn the wire back on now. Don't say anything you don't want on tape."

Christine finally gave in and slowly began getting dressed, knowing Gina would be relentless until she did. Gina left the bedroom and walked to the living room, where she turned the wire back on. "I'm here, guys." There were several sighs of relief from her co-workers outside. "Listen, I'm taking Christine to St. Vincent Hospital. A man she had dated beat her up pretty badly. And oh, please run a criminal history on the guy; his name is Stan Masterson. I happen to know him and he's very angry with me. Who knows? Maybe he's connected to this somehow."

She walked back to the bedroom and found Christine dressed, sitting quietly on the bed. "Explain to me what's going to happen."

Gina stood in front of her and said, "We'll have you checked out at the Emergency Room. I'll call it in and an officer will come by to take your statement. They will take pictures of all your injuries, too. After you file charges against Stan, he will be arrested."

Christine quickly asked, "Wouldn't that just make him more angry with me?"

Gina answered honestly, "Most likely, yes. But he's done this to you once. Who's to say he wouldn't do it again and maybe worse the second time? Especially, if he knows you won't press charges."

Christine smiled and commented, "You certainly are persuasive. Do you always get people to see things your way?"

Gina laughed and answered, "Only on the good days."

They left the apartment and made their way to Gina's car. Gina scanned the area, but saw nothing irregular. The drive to the hospital was a short one. It was only a couple of miles away. Gina had noticed the van and Bob's car in the rear view mirror and she wondered what they must be thinking of all of this. She dropped off Christine at the entrance to the Emergency Room and saw to it she was attended to by the staff. She then moved her car and parked it in a nearby lot. While sitting in her car, she said, "We're going to need an officer to take her statement. Please call it in." She got out of the car and went back into the hospital. Christine was still in the lobby, filling out the insurance paperwork.

Gina sat down beside her and waited while she completed the forms. They then gave the paperwork to the nurse at the counter. "Someone will be right with you," said the nurse. The lobby wasn't too busy and within a few minutes, Christine's name was called. Christine slowly walked towards the nurse, leaving Gina to wait in the lobby. She fidgeted for about fifteen minutes before an officer entered the lobby. It was one she didn't recognize.

She stood up and introduced herself. "Hello, I'm Detective Gina Perry. The woman who was attacked is a friend of mine."

He replied, "I've heard your name; it's good to meet you. I'm Dan Garrison. I just transferred here from Dallas PD. Where is your friend?"

"She's in the examining room. I'll go check on her and tell her you're here."

She walked through the double doors and began down the hallway. She flashed her badge at a nurse and asked, "Where is Christine Bennett?"

The nurse answered, "Second room on the left." Gina proceeded to the door and knocked gently. The doctor came to the door and Gina identified herself as a detective and friend of Christine's.

Christine yelled, "Gina, come on in." The doctor said that would be fine.

As Gina walked into the room, the doctor stated, "I've taken some x-rays of her ribs. She has 2 fractured ribs on her right side. Fortunately, they didn't puncture a lung." Gina stood beside Christine, who sat sideways on the examining table. Christine shivered a little, as she had removed her shirt and the room was a bit chilly. The nurse whom Gina had questioned in the hall walked into the room carrying bandages.

The doctor began wrapping the bandages around Christine's midsection. He said, "You're going to have to take it easy. These ribs are going to take some time to heal. I'll put a bandage over that cut on your face. It's not that bad and can heal on its own without stitches. Your face is going to be sore, but only time can improve that. I'll prescribe some pain killers, too."

In a professional tone, Gina stated, "We need to get a picture of that cut before you bandage it. There's an officer waiting in the lobby to take her statement and take pictures of the injuries."

Christine begged, "Gina, can't you just tell the officer what I told you?"

"I'm sorry, but it has to come from you," Gina explained.

Christine persisted, "I really don't want to go through it all again with someone else. It's embarrassing enough. Can't you take my statement?"

Gina looked sincerely into Christine's distressed eyes and said, "I understand what you're saying, but think about it. Stan and I don't like each other, to say the least. If I take your statement and you file charges against him, there could be a conflict of interest. A defense attorney could say I had a vendetta against him and forced you to file charges. If we do anything wrong, he could get away with it. I've seen it happen many times. Look, it comes down to you. It's your decision whether you want to press charges or not. But you would be better off to file the report now than a couple days later. Because then your credibility may be questioned because you failed to report it right away. I'm not saying it's right, but that's the way it is."

Christine sat quietly for a moment and then said, "I know you're right. It's just not something I relish discussing again. But I'll do it. Will you stay with me for support?"

Gina smiled and answered, "Of course, I will."

The doctor finished bandaging her ribs and said, "I'll come back to bandage the cut when the officer leaves." He then left. As the nurse continued to tend to the injuries to Christine's face, Gina left the room to get Officer Garrison.

She found him sitting in the lobby reading "People" magazine. "She's ready for you," announced Gina. He picked up his notebook and camera lying on the seat beside him, stood up, and followed Gina. She gave him a very brief summary of what had happened. She had him wait outside the doorway of Christine's room, while she went in to make sure Christine was ready. The nurse had left and Christine was gingerly putting on her shirt. "He's ready when you are," said Gina.

Christine sarcastically added, "It's just my luck the officer would be a guy. He'll probably make me feel stupid for letting Stan into my apartment in the first place. Let's get this over with; go ahead and bring him in." Gina opened the door and brought Officer Garrison into the room. She introduced them to one another and then let him take control of the situation.

Officer Garrison had Christine explain what had happened, just as Gina had done earlier. The story was the same, yet Christine seemed a bit more disconnected from it. He asked her if she wished to press charges against Stan. Christine looked at Gina before responding, "Yes, I do." Christine gave him identifying information of Stan, as well as his home address and job site. He handed her the report.

"I need you to read the report for accuracy and then sign it," he said.

While Christine was busy reading, he took the camera out of its carrying case and began preparing a photograph log.

Christine said, "This is accurate," and signed the complaint.

Officer Garrison took the paperwork from her and said, "We need to take some pictures of your injuries now. The x-rays of your fractured ribs will show the damage to your right side. Let's start with an overall shot of your face and then I'll get some individual shots of the cut and bruises." Christine understood it would be valuable evidence in a court of law and nodded her head in agreement. Gina looked on, as Officer Garrison meticulously took photographs of her facial injuries and described the shots on the photograph log.

He then stopped and stated hesitantly, "Uh, I'm going to have to take a couple more pictures, Ms. Bennett."

Christine looked rather confused as she said, "So, go ahead." Officer Garrison looked uncomfortable as he looked over at Gina, who was well aware of the awkward situation at hand. Gina intervened and took the pressure off him, for which she received a grateful look of relief. Gina took a few steps forward, leaving her standing directly in front of Christine.

In a comforting manner, Gina explained, "Christine, he needs to take some pictures of the bite mark on your chest. It will just take a minute and then you'll be done. Okay?" Christine said nothing, but timidly began unbuttoning her shirt.

Gina added, "You don't have to take it completely off, just drape it over your shoulders, so he can get a clear picture of it." Christine closed her eyes as he took the necessary photographs. Gina then told her, "It's all over, Christine."

Christine slowly opened her drowsy eyes, but didn't move or say anything. She looked very lethargic and her body slowly leaned forward. Gina stepped in front of her, catching her before she fell to the floor. Gina tried to lay her back down on the bed, but Christine kept a tight grasp around Gina's mid-section. Officer Garrison gathered his reports and camera, shook Gina's hand while she was embracing Christine, and exited the room.

It was obvious Christine had already been given painkillers. Her body lay limp in Gina's arms, with her head resting on Gina's left shoulder. Christine mumbled, "I want to go home."

Gina answered, "I've got to get you dressed first and the doctor has to put a bandage on that cut." Gina separated them and balanced Christine in front of her, while pulling Christine's shirt back to its rightful position. Christine's body began to sway, so Gina carefully lowered her body onto the bed and arranged the pillow neatly under her head.

While this was going on, Christine stammered, "Gina, I'm cold." Gina looked down and saw goosebumps forming on Christine's arms and chest. She promptly buttoned Christine's shirt and glanced around the room in search of a blanket. Surprisingly, there were none in sight. Gina was wearing a windbreaker jacket to conceal her weapon in the small of her back. She quickly removed it and covered Christine's torso.

While waiting for the doctor to return, Gina spoke softly to her co-workers via the wire. "Listen, everyone. I can't leave Christine alone tonight. She's in pretty bad shape. I don't want to bring her to my place and subject her to any more danger, so I plan to stay the night at her apartment. I'm sorry to mess up the surveillance. Maybe we don't need to continue it tonight." The doctor walked into the room and Gina pretended she had been talking to Christine, even though Christine wasn't lucid.

The doctor walked over to Christine and she groggily looked up at him. He told her, "This will only take a minute." The nurse returned and helped the doctor bandage the cut on Christine's face.

The doctor informed Gina, "She's already been given some sedatives. I've written a prescription for some painkillers. Our pharmacy is upstairs, if you would like to pick them up now."

Christine mumbled, "In my purse, Gina." She took Christine's purse and went to the pharmacy, while they continued to work on Christine.

When she returned, Christine was alone, fast asleep. Gina walked down the hallway and found the nurse. "Is she ready to go now?" asked Gina.

"Yes," the nurse answered. "She should come back in a week to see how things are healing." Gina nodded and headed back to the room.

She hated to wake Christine, but had no choice. She gently touched Christine's shoulder and said, "I can take you home now." Christine slowly opened her eyes and tried to sit up. She quickly grabbed her right side and Gina helped her to a standing position. Gina put the windbreaker jacket on Christine, hung Christine's purse around her neck, and carefully helped Christine walk out of the hospital. She sat Christine down on a bench just outside of the Emergency Room and then hurried to the parking lot to get the car. She noticed the surveillance van parked a couple lots away, but didn't see Bob's car.

She drove to the hospital entrance and helped Christine into the car. Gina buckled her in and rushed around the car. As soon as Gina jumped into the driver's seat, her cell phone rang. She grabbed the phone from the glove compartment and answered hastily, "Hello."

Bob's familiar voice echoed, "Gina, we're going to continue the surveillance. I can't explain it, but I just have a bad feeling about tonight and want to see this through. You know how you're always talking about women's intuition. Well, let's call this men's intuition."

Gina asked, "How does everybody else feel about this watch?"

Bob was firm in his reply. "We all just want to make sure you're okay." Bob was a smart man. Gina could tell by his answer the others were not as keen about the plans, but he knew they might be able to hear his voice through the transmitter.

"We'll go with your instincts, Bob. Have you seen anything suspicious tonight?"

"No, not yet. I ran the criminal history on Stan Masterson. Back in 2004, he was charged with spousal abuse. His wife later dropped the charges. A few months after that, they separated and she had a restraining order against him until their divorce was finalized. He has no other history on file."

She commented, "That's very interesting. He won't get away with it this time."

Bob asked, "How is Christine?"

"She has two fractured ribs and he beat her face up pretty badly, but she'll be okay."

"We'll be here if you need us."

"Thanks, Bob," Gina said appreciatively. "Thanks to all of you." The conversation ceased and Gina continued the drive to Christine's apartment.

CHAPTER 11

Gina pulled into the parking lot at Christine's apartment building and visually surveyed the lot. She saw nothing abnormal. She helped Christine into the building and onto the elevator. As the elevator climbed, Gina encouraged Christine. "We're almost there. You can make it. Then you can go right to bed." The elevator arrived at the fourth floor and they made their way to the apartment. With Christine leaning against her, Gina unlocked the door with Christine's keys. They stepped inside, turned on the lights, and quickly locked the door behind them. They staggered back to the bedroom and Gina sat Christine down on the bed.

As Gina set the purse and prescription bag down on the nightstand, Christine fell backward onto the bed exhausted. Gina took off Christine's shoes while Christine stammered, "Thank you for being here, Gina. I don't know what I'd do without you."

"Let's hope you never find out. Besides, you've always been there for me. I'm going to stay here tonight. Now, let's get you more comfortable."

Gina went to the dresser drawers and found some pajamas. She helped Christine get changed and then tucked her in, cozily underneath the covers. Gina asked, "Can I get you anything?"

Christine replied, "No thanks; I'm fine."

Gina started to leave the room, but was halted by Christine's soft voice. "Can you stay with me until I fall asleep?"

"Of course, I can," she said softly. She removed her weapon from its hideaway in the small of her back and placed it on the nightstand. She laid down on the bed beside Christine and held her hand.

"I know it's over, but I'm still scared," Christine said.

Gina stroked her hair, "You have nothing to worry about. I'm right here and I won't let anything happen to you. Close your eyes and try to get some sleep." Christine sighed and then shut her eyes. Within a few minutes, Christine was sleeping peacefully.

Gina carefully let go of Christine's hand and got up from the bed. She gently closed the bedroom door and went to the kitchen. She poured herself a soda and began looking through the refrigerator for a snack. It occurred to her that with everything going on, she hadn't eaten anything tonight. While rummaging through the refrigerator, she heard a noise coming from the bedroom. She hurried back there, fearing Christine may have fallen out of bed. She swung the door open and burst into the room. She couldn't believe her eyes as she reacted to the situation by reaching for her weapon. But her hand only felt an empty space and her eyes darted to her gun, sitting on the nightstand.

Before her, his eyes met hers. It was Stan! He sat beside a fearful looking Christine, whose mouth was covered by one of his hands and the other held her chest to the bed. He pleaded, "I just want to talk to her. This doesn't concern you, so leave!"

"Let her go and we can talk about this," Gina calmly ordered.

He yelled, "Forget you, bitch! This is between us! I don't want to hurt her. I just want to apologize." As he bent down and whispered in Christine's ear, Gina dashed to the nightstand and grabbed her 9-millimeter.

She pointed it directly at Stan and commanded, "Slowly, raise your hands and step away from her." He didn't respond. Gina shouted, "Don't give me a reason to blow your head off! You know I'll do it!"

Upon hearing that, he slowly arose from the bed and took a step backward. "Turn around and put your hands on the wall," she ordered. Stan complied. At that very moment, she heard the front door being kicked in. Into the apartment, ran Bob and the three other detectives.

Bob brushed past Gina and furiously began frisking Stan. He found no weapons. Bob handcuffed Stan and read him his rights. Bob then turned to Gina, who was sitting on the bed comforting Christine.

Bob anxiously asked, "Is this our man?"

Gina replied, "This is Stan Masterson, the guy who beat her up earlier tonight. She just filed assault charges against him. He must have broken in while we were at the hospital and hid in the closet."

"Well, we can add breaking and entering to the list," Bob stated.

As senior detective, Bob began delegating tasks. "Officer Knight, please take her statement. Detective Logan and Rogers, please transport him to the station. You can use my vehicle for transport. Book him for assault and breaking and entering. Officer Knight and I will be along soon in the surveillance van. Nobody talk to him until I get there." Bob handed Logan the car keys and the pair led Stan out of the apartment. Bob stated, "I'm going to have a look around the apartment and then check outside." He proceeded to do just that, while Officer Knight went to the surveillance van to get some report forms. This left Gina and Christine alone in the bedroom.

Gina reassured Christine, "Everything is going to be okay. Just wait and see."

Christine retorted, "What if you hadn't been here?"

Gina answered, "You can't consume yourself with 'what if's!' Everything worked out and you're safe. I'm going to go get my soda from the kitchen. Do you want anything?"

"A glass of water, please."

Gina walked to the kitchen and took a long drink of soda. She then poured a glass of water for Christine. Officer Knight returned and they walked to the bedroom. As Gina handed Christine the glass of water, she introduced her to Officer Pam Knight.

Gina asked, "Would you like something to drink, Pam?"

"No thanks, I've already had a coffee and two sodas tonight in the van."

Pam began to question Christine about what had happened. Christine simply stated, "There's not much to tell. He beat me up earlier tonight, as you already know. When we got back from the hospital, I went to sleep. I woke up when he put his hands over my mouth. I tried to scream to get Gina's attention, but couldn't. He kept saying he was sorry for what had happened earlier. I squirmed and tried to get away, almost knocking him off the bed. Then Gina came in. I'm sure you heard all of that."

Officer Knight asked, "Does he have a key to the apartment?" Christine shook her head.

Gina added, "He must have jimmied the lock on the front door and waited for her to return. Then he probably heard my voice at the door and hid in the bedroom closet until I went to the kitchen. I heard a noise and came back here. I saw him sitting on the bed beside her, with one hand covering her mouth and the other holding her down. I reached for my weapon, but realized I had left it on the nightstand. When he leaned down to whisper in her ear, I went for it and then had him assume the position. We'll have all that on tape."

They heard Bob enter the apartment and Gina left the bedroom. She found Bob working on the front door. One of the hinges had come off when he kicked the door in. The chain lock was also broken. He saw Gina and asked, "Do you know where she keeps a screwdriver?" Gina went to the kitchen and began digging through the drawer on the end. It was the hodgepodge drawer, the drawer we all have, the one with all the things we don't know what to do with.

She found various tools and asked Bob, "Do you need a Phillips or flathead?"

"Phillips," he replied.

She pulled one out of the drawer and handed it to him. She held the door in place, while he turned the hinge screws back into place. Bob then repaired the chain lock. He opened the door and pointed to the lock on the doorknob.

"See the scratches. This is where he picked the lock. She needs to have a deadbolt added."

Gina nodded and said, "I'll talk to her about it. Are you going to interrogate Stan tonight?"

"Yes, I am. It's probably best if you stay here with Christine. I'll get Logan or Rogers to sit in. Gina, how do you know Stan?" Gina went on to explain how he had come on to her at the construction site and later, how he felt she turned Christine against him.

Bob's look became very serious as he asked, "Could he be the man we're looking for?"

"I doubt it, but anything is possible. He is of the same physical description and he does hate me, but I've never known him to carry a weapon. If he was our guy, why would he just beat Christine up and leave? Secondly, why would he return to apologize? It just doesn't fit with the other attacks."

"Maybe, that's why he did it," Bob theorized. "Hopefully, he'll want to talk to me tonight. If he wants an attorney, I'll interview him in the morning. If it's okay with you, I'm going to call off the surveillance tonight. It's already midnight and I don't think anything else is going to happen. Who knows? Maybe it's over. Maybe Stan is our man. Or maybe Timbers was behind all of it and now that he's dead, no one would carry out his wishes because they wouldn't be paid. I'll meet you in the office in the morning. Call me if anything happens."

Officer Knight walked out of the bedroom and announced she had finished taking Christine's statement. She and Bob said their good-byes and exited the apartment. Gina locked the door and wedged a chair under the doorknob. She went back to the bedroom and found Christine kneeling on the floor. She saw Gina and said wearily, "I was trying to get to the bathroom, but got dizzy and fell down." Gina helped her up and walked her to the bathroom. Gina closed the door to give her some privacy and waited in the hallway. They spoke through the door.

Gina asked, "Are you feeling any pain? Do you need to take another painkiller?"

Christine answered, "No, I'm not feeling anything right now, other than dizziness."

Gina heard the sound of the toilet being flushed and a moment later, Christine opened the door. Gina walked beside Christine, with her arm around Christine's waist. They stumbled a bit, before reaching the bed. Gina pulled the covers back and helped her into bed. Gina then went into the bathroom and removed all of the monitoring devices.

She returned to the bedroom, laid down beside Christine and said, "Let's try this again." Christine gave a half smile and her eyelids drooped. Within a few minutes, not only was Christine asleep, but so was Gina.

Meanwhile, Bob and Officer Knight arrived at the station. Bob told her as soon as she typed up the statements, she could go home. He also released Detective Rogers for the night. He asked Detective Logan to sit in on the interrogation with Stan Masterson. Logan then called downstairs and asked a jailer to bring Stan to the detective division. Within five minutes, the jailer stepped off the elevator, leading a handcuffed, cocky-looking Stan.

The jailer showed Stan to the interview room; Bob and Logan followed. The jailer sat Stan down in a chair and waited outside the room. Bob and Logan sat opposite Stan at the table.

Bob said, "You've been read your rights. Do you wish to have an attorney present at this time?"

Stan stated matter-of-factly, "No. I have nothing to hide."

Bob and Logan were both a little surprised by Stan's remark. Bob set a tape recorder down on the table and said, "Then you won't mind if we record this?"

"No," Stan replied.

Bob turned the tape recorder on and began, "It is April 11th, 2006, at 12:45 AM. I, Detective Bob Wilson, along with Detective Paul Logan, am about to question Stan Masterson, in reference to an assault and breaking and entering. Mr. Masterson has been read his rights and wishes to waive his right to counsel at this time. Is this correct, Mr. Masterson?" Stan nodded his head up and down.

Bob explained, "I need you to answer me verbally for the recorder."

Stan said, "Yes, it's correct."

Bob continued the inquiry. "You've been charged with assault and breaking and entering. Tell us what happened."

Stan leaned back in his chair and then said, "Me and my girlfriend, Christine, got into an argument. Things got out of hand and I lost my cool. Yes, I did hit her. But I went back later to tell her I was sorry. I picked the lock on her door and waited for her to get back."

Bob asked for more details. "How many times did you hit her and where?"

Stan shrugged his shoulders and answered, "Hell, I don't know how many times. I was kind of out of it. I mean, she made me so angry I didn't even know what I was doing. I remember hitting her in the face, though."

Bob inquired, "What were you arguing about?"

"Oh, you know how women are," Stan responded. "They can turn anything into a big deal and want to stop seeing you." Stan chuckled and Bob smiled, in the hopes of gaining his confidence. Stan continued, "You see, I can't be happy with one woman. There's too many others out there to tempt me. But that doesn't make me a criminal, does it?"

Bob asked, "Isn't it true you made unwanted sexual advances towards my partner, Detective Perry, and she told Christine about it?"

Stan smirked and said, "You can't blame a guy for trying to get some, now can you?"

Bob changed the subject. "Look, Stan, you just told us when you got angry with Christine, you were out of it and didn't even know what you were doing." Stan nodded his head in agreement. Bob persisted, "Have there been other times this happened and maybe it went a little further?"

"What are you getting at?" Stan asked.

Bob carefully chose his words and asked in a leading manner, "Maybe there were other times when you were trying to 'get some' and the woman changed her mind, leaving you very angry?"

Stan smirked, "Look, man. I take what's mine. You take a woman out and make her feel special. She flirts and smiles at you all evening. Then you get her home and she doesn't want to put out. Who's the victim?"

Thoughts raced through Bob's mind as he asked, "Have you ever wanted a woman so much that you followed her around?"

Stan sat up in his chair and stated, "I don't know for sure what you're getting at, but I'm no stalker or rapist! Yes, I lost my temper and hit Christine tonight, but it was just an accident."

As a test of his honesty, Bob questioned, "Have you ever hit another woman?"

Stan casually answered, "Just my ex-wife and she deserved it. The bitch just couldn't keep her mouth shut for one minute. Look, guys, I'd love to sit here and chat with you all evening, but I'm kind of tired. I'd be happy to talk with you tomorrow with my attorney."

Logan forcefully asked, "I thought you had nothing to hide?"

"I don't. Do you, boys?" Stan sarcastically replied.

Logan got in Stan's face and Bob quickly pulled Logan backward into the chair. Bob stood up and opened the door. "Jailer, get him out of here." The young jailer entered the room and escorted Stan back to a cell, where he would wait until morning to go before the judge.

Back in the interview room, the conversation continued between Bob and Logan. Bob explained to the younger detective, "He asked for his attorney. We can't ask him any more questions after that. We've already got him for assault and breaking and entering. But we've got nothing else on him. Just because he's an asshole, doesn't mean he's a murderer. Don't get me wrong. He's still an unofficial suspect."

Logan acknowledged, "I understand what you're saying. But guys like him are a walking threat to all women. It's hard to sit still and listen to his smug attitude. I'm sure he comes off totally different around women, at least initially."

Bob added, "Oh, I'm sure he's a smooth talker with the ladies. He wants them to like him. He doesn't care what other men think of him."

The pair of detectives stepped out of the room and walked to their desks. Bob locked the tape recorder in his desk and said, "Let's go home and get some sleep."

They left the building and parted to go to their cars. The evening had not gone exactly as they had planned, but they did have a man in custody. He could be their man. Even if he wasn't, he deserved to be locked up for what he had done to Christine. So, in that respect, the surveillance had been successful. They could only hope Chief Buchanon would see it from the same perspective.

CHAPTER 12

Gina's day began with the sound of a ringing phone. She opened her eyes, half-wondering where she was. She looked around the room and realized she was at Christine's apartment. She rolled over, picked up her cell phone from the nightstand, and answered, "Hello."

Bob replied, "Good morning, Gina. I just wanted to set up a time to meet you at your place this morning before going to the station. I don't want you going in there alone."

"I'll meet you there in a half hour, if that's okay."

He answered, "That will work. I'll meet you in the parking lot." She agreed and hung up the phone.

She got up and went to the kitchen, where she found Christine making toast. "How are you feeling?" Gina asked.

"Sore," Christine replied. "I need to call work and let them know I won't be coming in, but I don't look forward to telling them what happened."

Gina said, "I could call for you, if you want me to."

"I appreciate it. But that would just be taking the easy way out. I'll do it."

Gina hugged her and said, "I'm so proud of you. It took a lot of courage for you to press charges. It was the right thing to do, even though it was very difficult. Actually, I've come to learn that the harder of two choices is generally, the right one."

Christine asked, "Would you like some toast?"

"No, thanks. I'm just going to use the bathroom and then head over to my place. Bob is meeting me there. He's worried someone may have broken in last night and could be there or have left some kind of message. I'll clean up there and then go in to work."

Gina left the kitchen and Christine got up the nerve to call her supervisor. Christine briefly told her what had happened and that she would be unable to work for a few days. As Christine hung up the phone and gave a sigh of relief, Gina opened the bathroom door and walked into the living room.

Gina asked, "Well, how did it go?"

"Pretty well," Christine answered. "She told me to take all the time I need."

"I'm glad; you're going to need some time to recuperate. The nurse told me you needed to come back in a week to have everything checked. You'll be fine, Christine." Gina headed for the door.

Christine said with sincerity, "I can't thank you enough for all you've done."

Gina replied, "You've always been there for me. Just get some rest and I'll call you later." The two women parted at the door and Gina heard Christine lock the door behind her.

She hurried to her car and drove home, where she found Bob waiting in the parking lot. They both got out of their cars and walked towards one another. Gina asked, "So how did the interview go with Stan?"

Bob shook his head while saying, "I'm glad Christine wants nothing to do with him. He's a bona fide loser. He thinks of himself as such a ladies' man, but he has the mental attitude of a teenage boy. He admitted to hitting Christine and his now ex-wife, but nothing more. You can listen to the tape today."

They made their way to her apartment and she unlocked the door. Bob stepped in front of her, with his weapon drawn. Gina followed suit. They carefully went through each room, but found nothing.

They holstered their 9 millimeters and Gina said, "You really thought someone was going to be here."

"I wanted to be sure," Bob admitted. "Yes, Dwayne Timbers is dead and if he had ordered the hits, they probably wouldn't be honored. And yes, Stan Masterson is in lockup. I'm just not sure he has anything to do with it. He is wicked, but is he intelligent enough to pull it off? I can see he has animosity for you and other women who have rejected him, but how would that connect him to Denise Steidman?"

"I don't know," she replied. "I just hope he leaves Christine alone." She paused for a moment's reflection and then said, "I'm going to take a quick shower. You can go ahead to the station."

He said resolutely, "I can wait. It's not a problem."

He sat down on the couch and turned the television on, while Gina made her way to the bathroom. He watched the morning news until Gina returned and said she was ready to go. They left her apartment and headed outside. They drove to the station without incident. They walked into the building and took the elevator upstairs to the detective division.

Upon arriving at their desks, Chief Buchanon bellowed, "Wilson and Perry, in my office now!" They immediately followed the Chief into his office. "Close the door behind you," he said. They all sat down and Chief Buchanon began, "I've already spoken with Logan and Rogers about last night. Do you two have any idea how much it costs to run a surveillance? Let me tell you, it's costly to pay overtime for five employees. If it produces results, it's worth it. If we screw it up, it looks like a waste of the taxpayers' money. Perry, how can you justify having them follow you while you take care of personal matters?"

Gina hesitated and then responded, "Sir, if this guy had been following me, he could have planned his attack at the hospital or at Christine's."

Bob intervened. "As senior detective, it was my call, not hers. As a matter of fact, she suggested we all go home sooner, but I disagreed. Chief, I understand what you're saying, but it wasn't a total loss. It was a good thing we were there to arrest Stan Masterson. I also consider him a possible suspect on this case, sir."

The Chief placed his left hand under his chin and sat in silence for a moment before saying, "I'm glad you and your friend are okay, Perry. But we need to make some headway on this case. Get out there and follow all the leads you have. Make it happen!"

"Are we continuing the surveillance?" Bob asked.

Chief Buchanon looked at Gina and said, "Not at this time. I'm assigning an officer to guard you when you're at home and I want a detective following you whenever you leave your apartment during off duty hours. Wilson, you oversee that." Bob nodded as the Chief continued, "This guy never seems to attack during the day; he must have a day job. I'm still not convinced Timbers wasn't connected to this. But we won't know unless there's another attack."

"Christine is pretty shaken by all this," Gina informed. "I'm going to stay at her place one more night. Is that going to be a problem if I have an officer guarding me, Chief?"

"No, I'll just have the officer stand guard there."

She said, "Thanks, sir," and they walked out of the office. Gina and Bob sat down at their desks, which faced one another.

Bob handed her a tape recorder and headset while saying, "Here's the interview with Stan Masterson." She took it and immediately began listening to it. While doing so, she noticed Bob received a phone call. The conversation lasted about the same length of time as the interview with Stan. As he hung up the phone, she took off the headset.

Bob said, "That was Mark Steidman. I updated him on the case. He told me the visitation is tomorrow night at 7 PM and the funeral is at 10 AM on Friday."

Gina sadly stated, "I'm going to both the visitation and funeral. I want to pay my respects and also check out the crowd."

"That's a good idea. I'll go with you. You never know who may show up."

Bob then pointed to the tape and asked, "So, what did you think of old Don Juan?"

She replied, "He's the same asshole I always knew he was. I'm just sorry Christine got involved with him. I'm also worried about his arraignment today. With no prior convictions, there's a good chance he will be released on bond. After all, we can't connect him to any other attacks."

"Do you think he would go after Christine again?"

Gina sighed and said, "He's not the type to just let it go. That's part of the reason I want to stay with her again tonight. But, you never know. Maybe after being held overnight in jail, he'll want to stay away from her."

"So what did you have in mind for this afternoon?" Bob asked.

Gina pulled out her notebook and stated, "Some of Denise's co-workers gave me some names of Denise's friends outside of work. I'd like to talk with them and see if she had any enemies or if anything unusual had been going on."

Bob said, "Sounds like a good idea. I'll go with you. Let's go get something to eat, first." She agreed, but said she first had to call Christine and see if she needed anything. She called Christine and told her that she planned to be over after work. Christine sounded happy about that and said everything was fine. Gina hung up the phone and they left the station.

They had lunch at a nearby pizza place and spent the rest of the afternoon talking to Denise Steidman's friends. They all seemed like wonderful people, who were deeply shocked by the loss of their friend. None of them knew her to have any enemies. She lived an average life with no apparent problems that were unlike anyone else's. She and Mark had their disagreements, mostly over having children and her job, but no one viewed it as a major problem. They were a happy couple who looked forward to spending the rest of their lives together.

Gina and Bob returned to the station, only to find out from Logan that Stan had pled guilty at his arraignment and bonded out. Gina asked, "What time was he released?"

"About an hour and a half ago," Logan informed.

It was already 4:30 and Gina was anxious to go to Christine's. "Bob, can you take me home now?" asked Gina. He nodded and the two quickly left the station.

While driving to Gina's apartment, Bob said, "I want to go in with you and check things out."

She casually said, "Whatever." Her mind was focused on Christine and she hoped Stan would just leave her alone.

They pulled into the lot and walked toward the building, checking Gina's car on the way. There were no notes or damage done to the car. They walked into the building, got onto the elevator, and eagerly awaited the third floor. The elevator bell dinged and the doors opened. They stepped out and headed down the hallway, immediately spotting Officer Brooks standing guard outside of Gina's apartment. She asked him, "How long have you been here?"

"Not long, the Chief sent me about half an hour ago." Gina explained she was just going to pack an overnight bag and was then leaving for Christine's.

All three carefully entered her apartment, but found nothing disturbed. Bob decided to leave, since Officer Brooks was with her. "Call me if anything happens," he said. She told him she would and the two parted.

Gina locked the door behind him and Officer Brooks waited in the hallway. Gina hurried to the bedroom and rapidly threw some clothes and toiletries into a small overnight bag. As she picked up the bag and walked out of the bedroom, there was a knock at the door.

She heard Officer Brooks say, "Detective Perry, there's a man here to see you."

She quickly walked to the door and looked through the peephole. It was Ted. She unlocked the door and told Officer Brooks it was okay. Even though she was in a hurry to get to Christine's, she showed Ted into the apartment, sorry she had been abrupt with him last night. She had to talk to him now, or he might think she wasn't interested.

Ted saw the overnight bag sitting on the living room floor and asked, "Are you going somewhere?"

"Yes, I'm going over to a girlfriend's," she answered.

Ted looked rather disappointed and said, "That's a shame. I was going to invite you over for dinner. Maybe some other time."

She reached for his hand and said, "I would like that. I'm sorry about last night. Things are just pretty crazy right now. On top of some man stalking me, my best friend, Christine, was beat up by her ex-boyfriend last night. I would love to have dinner with you, but she needs me. I hope you understand."

He smiled and said, "Of course, I do. But when things settle down for you, let's go away together for a few days. I have a friend who owns a cabin in the woods at a place called 'The Water's Edge,' just a couple hours from here. It overlooks a lake and the scenery is just breathtaking. Promise me, you will at least think about it."

She grinned and said, "I already am."

He hugged her and said, "I guess I better let you get going." They parted and he opened the door for her. She stepped out into the hallway and he followed.

"Take good care of her," Ted said to the officer. Gina and Officer Brooks headed down the hallway, as Ted stepped into his apartment and closed the door.

They walked to their cars and she drove to Christine's. With her overnight bag in hand, Gina walked into the building, with Officer Brooks at her side. They waited impatiently for the elevator and finally, it arrived. Several people got off before they were able to get on. When the bell dinged for the fourth floor, Gina bolted out and raced to Christine's door. She knocked, but got no response. She listened intently, but heard nothing. She yelled, "Christine, is everything okay in there?" Just as she and Officer Brooks were getting ready to kick the door in, she heard the locks being unbolted and the door opened halfway. Christine peered around the door and looked very relieved.

"I'm so glad you're here, Gina! Stan came by a little while ago. I thought you were him."

Gina noticed Christine staring at Officer Brooks and introduced them. She described Stan to him and told him not to let Stan near the apartment. Gina then entered the apartment and locked the door behind them. In some ways, Christine looked worse than she did last night. The majority of her face was bruised and turning various shades of black, blue, and yellow. She walked very slowly to the couch, while holding her right side gently. Her eyes were red and it was obvious she had been crying. She wore a pair of blue shorts and a t-shirt.

"What happened when he came by?" Gina asked.

"I sat still and pretended I wasn't here," Christine replied. "He didn't say anything."

Gina asked, "Then how did you know it was him?"

"I looked out the window and saw him leave," Christine answered. "So that's it, huh? I go through all that, press charges, and he's out the next day. What good did it do, Gina?"

"I know how unfair it seems," Gina conceded. "But he'll get what's coming to him. I was surprised he pled guilty at the arraignment. He's probably hoping for probation or minimal jail time. Or maybe, he's just plain stupid." Gina changed the subject, as she could see it was upsetting Christine. "So how are you feeling?"

"Not as bad as I look," Christine replied. "Although, the pain killers have me pretty doped up and I've slept most of the day."

"Have you eaten anything?" Christine shook her head no. Gina stood up and walked to the kitchen, where she began surveying the cupboards and refrigerator. "You have all the makings for spaghetti. How does that sound?"

Christine smiled and said, "That sounds good. Let me help you."

Gina stopped her from getting up and said, "You just relax and let me do it. I've been on painkillers before and I know how dizzy they made me. You don't need to be doing anything." Christine thanked her and asked how her day had gone. Gina briefly explained what was going on with the case, but told Christine not to worry about it.

Christine commented, "You're my friend and I worry about you. Sometimes, I think you worry more about me than yourself, Gina. You don't have to spend the night. I'll be fine."

Gina insisted, "I'm going to stay here tonight. But tomorrow, I just might have other plans, Christine." Her wide smile was the giveaway.

Christine pleaded, "Come on, Gina. Tell me what's going on. You know everything in my life, now open up to me. It's your neighbor, Ted, isn't it? You slept with him!"

Gina finally got a word in and answered her. "No, I haven't slept with Ted. I mean, yes, I slept in the same bed with him the night Denise Steidman was murdered. I was really lonely and scared. But nothing happened." Christine arose from the couch and walked to the kitchen, where she sat down at the table.

Gina continued to cook as Christine asked sincerely, "What's holding you back?"

Gina shrugged her shoulders and answered, "I don't know. I guess I'm just afraid of getting hurt again. Think back to how strongly I felt about Derick and look what happened with that. And before Derick, there was Brian. Remember how he changed? They all seem so wonderful in the beginning and then everything seems to change after you sleep with them. How do I know Ted would be any different?"

Christine stated honestly, "You don't know. Look at Stan and what's happening to me now. I know what you're saying. Neither of us have had much luck when it comes to men. But you're going to have to let your guard down completely if you're ever going to find someone who will truly love you. How do you feel about Ted?"

"I really find him appealing, both physically and mentally. That's a combination you don't find very often."

"Does he know how you feel?"

"No!" Gina blurted.

"If you want my advice, you should tell him before it's too late. Oh, I almost forgot to ask. Have you heard from Derick or has he accepted the breakup?"

"He's called, but I haven't spoken with him. I think he will let it go now."

Gina finished preparing their dinner and piled spaghetti on three plates, one for Christine, one for herself, and one for Officer Brooks. Gina invited him in, but he thought it best to stay in the hallway. She pulled out a chair from the kitchen and handed him a plate of spaghetti, along with a soda. He was very appreciative. They all enjoyed the meal and the night passed quickly. Gina and Christine watched television and then Christine decided she would go to bed.

Gina said, "I'll be fine out here on the couch. Don't worry about it. Let me know if the television is too loud."

"Thanks again for all your help," Christine said, as she headed to the bedroom.

Gina went to the bathroom and changed into shorts and a t-shirt. She stayed up a little while longer, but then turned the television off and placed a chair under the doorknob of the front door, just as an extra precaution. She then placed some sheets on the couch and laid down.

Meanwhile, he sat alone, planning his next move. He wanted her more than the others and he would soon prove it to her. But he would have to be patient. After all, it wasn't worth getting caught. That would mean the end to an era and he couldn't bear the thought. It was his responsibility to rid the world of women like her and he took it very seriously. He was the chosen one and he had known it for a long time.

CHAPTER 13

Heavy footsteps coming from the upstairs apartment awakened Gina. She got up, walked to the door, and looked through the peephole. There had been a shift change, leaving a new officer sitting in the chair in the hallway. Gina walked to the bedroom and peeked in, only to find Christine still sleeping. She walked back to the living room and picked up her bag, before heading to the bathroom. After taking a shower and getting dressed, she opened the bathroom door and heard Christine talking to someone. She raced to the bedroom and saw Christine talking on the phone. Christine was saying, "I told you, I don't want to see you again! It's over!"

Gina grabbed the phone from Christine's hand and said, "Leave her alone or I'll have you arrested for harassment!" Without uttering a word, Stan hung up the phone.

Gina asked Christine, "Did he threaten you?"

"No," she answered. "He just kept saying he was sorry and how he missed me."

Gina fervently said, "No way! You can't be feeling sorry for him!"

"Part of me does," Christine admitted. "I know it sounds insane, but it's true. He sounded so sincere."

"Of course, he does," Gina responded. "He's trying to convince you it won't happen again, but I assure you, it will. This guy is a total loser. You should hear how he talks about women when he's talking to men. It's pure filth! You should stay as far away from him as possible."

Christine added, "I didn't say I wanted him back. I just said I felt a little sorry for him."

"If he calls again, just hang up. Don't talk to him at all. Do the same if he comes by. If he won't leave, call the police and tell them he's harassing you. A patrol car could get here faster than me, but call me, too. If necessary, you can get a restraining order against him." Christine nodded in agreement.

Gina said, "I have to get going. Do you think you'll be okay by yourself tonight?"

"Yes, I'll be fine. You should spend some time with Ted."

"Why don't we go out for dinner and a movie tomorrow night?" Gina suggested. "I'm sure you'll be ready to get out of this apartment by then."

Christine groggily said, "On a Friday night? Wouldn't you rather spend it with Ted?"

Gina stated cheerily, "I'll see him tonight. Friday will be a girls' night out. Okay?"

Christine smiled and finally said, "Okay." Gina was glad. Too much time in the apartment would only depress Christine and make her think more about Stan and men, in general. Gina left the apartment, got in her car, and drove directly to the station. The officer followed her. She thought about going to her place first to check things out, but decided against it.

As she arrived at the station, it began to rain lightly. She ran into the building and made her way upstairs. She immediately spotted Bob. He was grinning widely and his face beamed with excitement. He didn't even say "hello" or "good morning."

He anxiously said, "I have something to tell you." Gina leaned back against his desk, already knowing what he was about to say. She had promised Lisa she would keep the pregnancy a secret, so she prepared to look surprised. She played along.

"Well, what is it?"

He smiled deliriously as he announced, "I'm going to be a father again!"

She gave him a big hug and said, "That's wonderful! I'm so happy for both of you."

"She told me last night. It really took me by surprise and I didn't know what to think at first. I'm not a young man anymore. But I realized how much I love my wife and son. Having another child would only bring more happiness into our lives, no matter how old we are."

Gina added, "Lisa and Kyle are very lucky to have you and this baby will be, too."

Bob thanked her for her kind words and then changed the subject. "How did it go last night?"

"It was pretty uneventful," she responded. "Stan called this morning, trying to convince Christine he was sorry for hitting her. And you know what the sad part is? She felt a little sorry for him. I guess it was a good lesson for me. We constantly talk to women who have been beaten by their husbands or boyfriends and these women stay with the guy because they love them. They risk everything to be with someone who treats them like that. I never understood it and still don't. But now it's a friend of mine who is an educated woman whom I would have thought would have known better. Are we, as women, so desperate to find a man, that we're willing to sacrifice our own well being? I certainly hope it hasn't come to that!"

Bob simply said, "Gina, the day I see you stay with a man who beats you is the last day I want to see." She smiled at Bob in appreciation, for he was among the last of the good guys.

Logan came over to their desks and smiled as he said, "I hate to interrupt this philosophical conversation. I don't hear much of that around here. But I have the results from the lab regarding the Steidman homicide."

Gina quickly changed mental gears and asked, "What did they find?"

"Not a whole lot, I'm afraid. We dusted the whole place for prints and only found a few smudged latents. But the lab couldn't identify them because they were unclear. No one else's blood was found at the scene. As for the method of entry, the screen in the living room had been cut by some type of knife, but they were unable to determine a specific kind."

"Is that it?" Bob asked.

"Unfortunately, yes," Logan replied. "It was all a bunch of dead ends. This guy is very cautious and doesn't leave anything behind. Do you guys have any leads you want me and Rogers to check out today?"

"That's the problem," Bob replied. "We don't have much to go on. Gina and I are going to talk to some of Steidman's family. We've already covered her work and close friends. You and Rogers could run down some of our snitches on the street and see if they've heard anything. That would be a big help."

"Consider it done," Logan stated. He walked away, informed Rogers of their assignment, and they left the building.

Bob asked Gina, "Are you ready to go?"

She nodded and stood up saying, "We better tell the Chief what's going on first."

Bob agreed, "You're right. As each day passes without an arrest, the more irritable and uneasy he becomes."

The two detectives went into the Chief's office and briefed him on the case. As expected, he wasn't a happy man. But as Bob pointed out, it had only been a week since Gina was attacked and just three days since the Steidman homicide. They assured Chief Buchanon they were doing their best and apprised him of their plans for the day. Gina also told him that they were going to attend the Steidman visitation that night. The Chief told them he wanted a daily update on the case and they nodded their heads in acknowledgment. They left his office, took the elevator downstairs, and walked to their car.

They spent the day talking to several of Denise Steidman's relatives, both on her side and Mark's side of the family. Denise's sister, Dana, was so upset she refused to talk with them, but everyone else was cooperative. None of them knew of anyone who would want to harm her. There didn't appear to be any real problems going on in her life.

Gina and Bob went back to the station to check in with Logan and Rogers. They hadn't had much success, either. They had spoken with several snitches, but none claimed to have known anything about the attack on Gina or the Steidman homicide. Whoever did it, wasn't bragging about it. Logan and Rogers told the snitches to let them know if they heard anything and there may be some cash in it for them. It was just going to take some time and Gina feared it may cost someone their life, maybe even her own.

After reviewing some files, Gina left for the day. She had been told Officer Brooks had just been assigned to her again and was on the way to her apartment. She drove home and as she pulled into her lot, Ted pulled in behind her. After they parked, he purposely waited at his Explorer, so he would not startle her like before. She got out of her car and walked over to him. "Hi, Ted. How was your day?"

"It went alright," he answered. "How about yours?"

She sighed before saying, "I've had better, but I've also had worse. Would it be presumptuous of me to ask for that raincheck of dinner tonight?"

He laughed and said, "Even if it was, I wouldn't care. I like a woman who knows what she wants."

They walked together up to their apartments and parted at his door. "I'll be over in just a minute," she told him. She was a bit surprised Officer Brooks wasn't there, but assumed he had gotten a call and would be along soon. She entered her apartment and looked in every room. Everything looked okay. She checked her answering machine; there were no messages. She combed her hair and left the apartment. As she was knocking on Ted's door, Officer Brooks stepped off the elevator.

He said, "I'm sorry I'm a little late; I had to work a traffic accident on the way over here."

She casually stated, "It wasn't a problem, really. I'm having dinner with my neighbor and then I'm going to the Steidman visitation. Detective Wilson will be picking me up." Just then, Ted opened his door and greeted them.

"Would you like a chair, officer?"

"Yes, thank you," he said. Ted brought a chair out from his kitchen and handed it to the officer. He and Gina then stepped inside his apartment and closed the door behind them.

Ted walked to the kitchen, where he had already begun cutting up vegetables. "I hope you like stir fry," he said. "I'm making chicken with fettuccine noodles, broccoli, and carrots. Normally, I put onions and peppers in it, but I remembered you don't like those."

She smiled and said, "It sounds great. What can I do to help?"

"You could cut up the carrots while I do the broccoli, if you want to," he answered. He pulled a knife from the butcher block and handed it to her. She took it and began slicing the carrots.

She glanced down at her watch; it was 5:20 PM. She said, "Unfortunately, I have to be somewhere at 7:00."

He jokingly said, "Do you have a hot date?"

She laughed and flirtatiously answered, "You mean after this one?"

He stopped cutting the broccoli and took a step towards her, knife in hand. She was enthralled by him and stood in silence. He set the knife down on the counter and slowly bent down to kiss her. She leaned towards him and their lips finally met. What began as a soft kiss quickly turned into a passionate embrace. He leaned against her, his weight pushing her against the wall. They kissed intensely, as his hands feverishly caressed her body.

Gina's heart pounded in her chest and her body felt enflamed. She thought, Where has this man been all my life? It was more than simply lust. It was an overpowering sense of destiny that their minds and bodies should meet. Their passion was interrupted by the sound of Gina's knife dropping on the kitchen floor. She jumped, startled by the sound, only half realizing her hand had let it go. They parted and Ted picked up the knife.

He jokingly said, "It seems you've dropped something." She laughed, as he set the knife down on the counter.

He spoke, "Well, it appears your feelings have changed." She couldn't hide it any longer. Her body had already shown him her true feelings.

"Yes, I have feelings for you. I just wanted to be sure how I felt, before I said anything to you."

"And are you sure now?" Ted asked.

"I'm positive!" she said.

He hugged her closely and said, "I've waited a long time to hear you say that. I feel very lucky to have you in my life. Now let's get dinner going, so you can make your appointment."

"I want to tell you where I'm going, so you don't get the wrong idea. I'd like to stay here longer, but it's work related."

He cut her off by saying, "Don't worry about it. We have all the time in the world, right?" She agreed and continued to help prepare the meal.

It wasn't long before the food was ready and they enjoyed a quiet dinner together. She really had to force herself to leave; she was having such a good time.

They kissed good-bye at the door and he asked her, "When can I see you again?"

"I'm not sure," she replied. "I have plans with my friend, Christine, tomorrow night. It's sort of a girls' night out kind of thing, or I would invite you to join us."

"I guess it would be presumptuous to ask you to come by when you get home tonight," he said.

"Let's not rush things, Ted."

"Do you feel safe by yourself with everything going on?" he asked.

"I have Officer Brooks in the hallway," she answered.

He quickly said, "But you had an officer there last time and look what happened." Gina didn't say a word and then Ted said, "I'm sorry. I shouldn't have said that. I just don't want anything to happen to you."

"I'm very independent, Ted. I'm not going to run to you every time there's a problem. I appreciate your concern, but I'll be fine." He smiled and gave her a quick peck on the cheek.

She opened the door and Officer Brooks stood up. She opened her own door while saying, "I just want to check my answering machine for messages. Bob should be here any minute." She quickly walked in and learned there were no messages.

As she exited her apartment, Bob stepped out of the elevator down the hall and asked "Are you ready to go?"

"Yes, I'm ready. Officer Brooks, you can go back out on patrol now."

All three went downstairs and to their cars. Officer Brooks waved as he pulled out of the lot in front of them. Gina and Bob didn't talk much on the way to the funeral home. When they arrived, Bob made no motion to get out of the car.

"I'm going to keep an eye on things out here," he said. "Let me know if you see anyone who looks out of place inside. Our boy may want to see all the grief he's caused."

She got out of the car and walked towards the funeral home. There were people waiting in line at the doorway. She proceeded to get in line and wait. The line was moving slowly. She was a bit uncomfortable being there. Everyone else seemed to know each other and she felt like an outsider. But she wanted to pay her respects and continued to tell herself she had a right to be there, just like all the others. At her place in line, she neared the casket and began feeling very nervous. Visions of Denise's mutilated body and Gina's name cut into her chest raced through her mind. But she tried not to think about it. She had to keep it together, at least for right now. She tried to occupy her mind with other things until she was the one facing the casket.

Gina walked up to her with teary eyes and stared solemnly at Denise. She quickly said a prayer and turned to face Denise's grieving family. First in line was her husband, Mark. He was trying to keep it together, but the pain was evident on his face. She shook his hand and offered her condolences once again. As he thanked her for coming, someone jerked her around by her shoulder and slapped her in the face. It was Denise's sister, Dana.

"You have no right being here!" she yelled. "Get the hell out!"

Mark intervened and said, "It's not her fault, Dana! She's doing everything she can to catch whoever did this!"

"It is her fault!" Dana shouted. "The asshole who did this carved her name in Denise's chest! He just used Denise to get to her!"

Gina replied, "I will do everything possible to catch this guy. I promise you. But I can't bring back your sister and for that, I'm sorry."

Gina pushed past Dana and the rest of the line of mourners. With all eyes on her, she hurried out the front door and began walking across the parking lot. She was stopped by the sound of someone calling her name. She turned around and saw Mark at the doorway.

He walked over to her and said, "She's just upset. She didn't mean what she said."

"Thanks, but I think she did," Gina replied. "I'm sorry my coming here upset her. I just wanted to pay my respects. Denise was a wonderful person whom I wish I had gotten to know better."

"I don't know how I'm going to live without her," he said with tears in his eyes and a wavering voice.

She touched his arm and said, "I meant what I said. I will do whatever it takes to catch whoever did this." He nodded and she continued, "I should let you know I'm coming to the funeral tomorrow, along with a few other detectives."

"I didn't realize she knew so many people in the police department," he stated.

She explained, "Not all of them knew her. But in a case like this, the perpetrator sometimes likes to see all the pain and suffering he's caused."

He looked away and then asked, "Are you saying whoever did this knew her?"

"Not necessarily, but it's a possibility. Or whoever did this could come back and watch the funeral from across the street or some other location. I've seen it happen."

"Well, I better get back in there," he said. He turned around and hurried into the building, leaving Gina standing there in a dismal daze.

She composed herself before walking over to the car. As she got in, Bob asked, "Is everything okay?"

She didn't answer him, but instead asked, "Have you seen anyone out of the ordinary?"

"No," he replied.

"Let's just call it a night, Bob."

He agreed and turned on the ignition. On the way home, flashbacks of the scene at the funeral home flooded her thoughts. She felt Dana's emotional pain wholeheartedly and began to wonder if she was, somehow, responsible. Maybe there was a clue she had overlooked or a lead she didn't pursue. But she had racked her brain and couldn't think of anything. Deep down, she thought about staking out John Utik's house, but realized it wasn't possible with an officer watching her every move. Maybe tomorrow during the day, she thought.

Back home, she began pouring two glasses of soda. A moment later, Bob came out of the bathroom and she handed him one of the glasses. He thanked her and then called the station to request that the officer return to Gina's apartment.

"I'll stay until the officer gets here," he said. "Are you sure you're okay? You don't look so good, Gina."

She explained what had happened at the visitation. Bob's response was very direct. "You've done everything humanly possible to catch this guy. It's not your fault! Don't let Dana get to you; she's just mourning the loss of her sister."

"I know. I'm just ready for us to catch a break on this case."

He said with certainty, "We will. Plus, the guy hasn't struck since Monday night when Dwayne Timbers was killed. Maybe it's over and we just don't know it yet."

She added, "Even if it was Timbers, we would still have to find the hitman. But at least the rest of it would stop."

Bob then changed the subject by discussing Lisa's pregnancy. It wasn't long before Officer Brooks arrived. Bob and Gina said goodnight and she locked the door behind him. She again propped a chair under the doorknob. At the very least, it would slow someone down a little or make more noise.

She drank the rest of her soda in front of the television and thought about what Ted had said. She was fortunate to be at Ted's the last time when Officer Kimble was hit over the head and the guy broke into her apartment. What if he came back tonight? She tried to calm down by telling herself she could handle whatever happened. She was truly scared, but didn't want Ted to become a safety blanket. This would all end soon and then they could start their relationship under calmer conditions when she was thinking more clearly. She really did like him and looked forward to spending more time with him.

She decided she should try to get some sleep. She knew tomorrow would be an emotionally draining day with the funeral. She changed into pajamas, washed up, and tucked herself into bed. Her mood was heavy, as she closed her eyes and desperately tried to forget about everything. It was a difficult task and would only get harder.

CHAPTER 14

She woke up several times that night and found herself looking through the peephole to see if an officer was still there. But he always was and she returned to bed. When morning came, she felt exhausted. She thought a cool shower might help her wake up and it did. She hurried off to work, with the officer following. When they arrived, she thanked him and they parted. She went upstairs to the detective division and he went to his sergeant in the patrol division.

Gina, who was wearing black pants, a white shirt, and a black suit jacket, approached Bob. He was sitting at his desk, with his head buried in paperwork. She said, "Morning, Bob."

He looked up at her and replied, "Good morning."

"You're still going to the funeral, right?" He nodded his head.

"So is Logan and Rogers," he added. "They'll just sit in the car and watch the surrounding area for anyone suspicious. You and I can check out the crowd inside." She agreed and they advised Chief Buchanon of their plans before they left.

On the way to the church, Gina tried to mentally prepare herself for the funeral. Every funeral she went to reminded her of the funeral of her parents, sister, and brother. She had sat in utter shock and despair, with all four caskets lined up in front of her. She had no family left to console her. She had sat with Christine and her parents in the front row. She remembered the sheer pain in her heart, the nausea in her stomach, and the seemingly inept ability of her lungs to provide her with enough air. On top of that, she felt an enormous amount of survival guilt and didn't understand why she had been spared. She thought the service would never end and wanted to just run out of there, but felt it would be disrespectful to her family. So instead, she held it together as best as she could, only losing it a few times and burying her face in her hands while sobbing uncontrollably. It was Christine's arms that had embraced her and comforted her in her time of dire need.

Bob's voice interrupted her thoughts. "Are you okay? You don't have to go in there, Gina." Her ears heard him, but her brain did not.

"I'm sorry, Bob. What did you say?"

"You don't have to go in there. Why put yourself through all that? You've been through enough."

She straightened up in the seat and said, "I'll be fine. Don't worry about me."

He frowned and knew it was a lost cause to try to convince her otherwise. They pulled into the church parking lot, which was already nearly full. She took a deep breath and then got out of the car.

As they walked towards the church and began climbing the steps, Gina said, "Let's find a seat near the back." He nodded and then opened the door for her. The familiar sounds of the organ ringing its death tunes permeated the grief-stricken air. Only a few whispers were heard, above the sniffling sounds, coughing, and men clearing their throats. Bob led Gina to the back row and they sat down.

They sat in silence, awaiting the start of the service. Gina stared blankly at the casket in the front of the church. She then furtively surveyed the crowd and saw several familiar faces, many of whom they had interviewed in the last few days. She also observed many members of the probation and parole department, as well as a few judges, including Judge Slocum. She recognized some others as lawyers, whom Denise had come into contact with on the job. No one really seemed to look out of place. It was apparent that she was loved and respected by many, as the enormous church was nearly filled to capacity.

After about five minutes, the service began. Unlike many other funerals Gina had been to, it was very personalized. Rather than quoting scriptures incessantly, the minister talked about Denise

Steidman as an individual, separate from all others who had died before her. The minister told stories of her life and the joy she had brought to others. The eulogy was given by her friend, Valerie Bruster, the one who had found her in the bedroom. Amidst tears and tissue breaks, Valerie spoke of a remarkable lady who was always helping others and trying to make the world a better place. She described her death as a brutal injustice, not only to Denise, but to all those who knew and loved her.

It left Gina feeling much closer to Denise. She quietly pulled out a tissue from her pocket and wiped her eyes. The organ played another woeful song, as the service ended. And so began the parade of people to the casket, to say their final good-byes. When Gina and Bob approached the casket, Dana started to get up, but was halted by her brother-in-law, Mark Steidman. Gina looked at Denise's body one last time and exited the church somberly.

Groups of people gathered in the parking lot, talking about lighter subjects such as the weather and sporting events. Gina and Bob stood next to each other amongst the crowd, but Gina remained silent. Bob suggested, "Maybe you should go away for the weekend with a friend and have some fun."

"I can't with all this going on. But Ted has invited me up to the lake at 'The Water's Edge.' I might go up there for a couple days when we catch this guy and everything settles down. But I can't right now."

Their conversation was interrupted by the approaching Judge Slocum. He walked up to Bob and they shook hands. "It's good to see you, Detective Wilson, although I wish it were under better circumstances. It's such a shame."

"Yes, it is," Bob replied.

Judge Slocum then turned to Gina and casually said, "Good day, Detective Perry."

"Good day, Judge."

Their attention turned to the pallbearers, who were carrying the casket down the church steps. The family followed and watched helplessly as the casket was slid into the back of the waiting hearse. The doors slammed and everyone moved to their cars to follow the procession. Gina and Bob were near the end of the line, which extended a couple of city blocks. The cemetery was not far away and everyone weaved through the cemetery trails until the hearse rolled to a standstill at the top of the hill.

Gina and Bob sat silently in the car until the pallbearers carried the casket to the open grave. They let everyone else follow it, before they stepped out of the car. They stood in the background and listened to the final prayer, which spoke of a better place with new beginnings. When the prayer ended, Gina started to walk away from the crowd. Bob followed her to the car.

They both got in and Bob asked, "Do you want to go back to the station now?"

"I guess," she replied soberly. Bob tried to make casual conversation on the way, but Gina wasn't interested. Her thoughts were on much deeper subjects.

They pulled into the station and got out of the car. Without a word, they went into the building and rode the elevator upstairs. They made it to their area and Gina put her purse down on her desk. She then went to the women's restroom, just down the hall. Bob stood there bewildered, not knowing what to do. He decided if she didn't come out in a few minutes, he would check on her. The funeral had obviously upset her a great deal, much more than she was willing to admit to him.

He waited impatiently, but ten minutes had passed and Gina had not returned. He walked to the women's restroom and knocked on the door while yelling, "Gina, is everything alright?"

"I'm fine," she yelled back. "Just give me a few minutes." Bob stood at the door, not knowing if she truly was fine or simply said it to get him to go away. He walked back to his desk and saw Officer Knight talking with Logan about some reports. Bob hurried over to them and asked her to check on Gina. Of course, she said she would.

Officer Knight walked down the hall and entered the restroom, with Bob waiting outside the door. She found Gina sitting on the couch in a distant trance. Knight sat down beside her and asked, "Your partner is pretty worried about you. Are you okay?"

"No, but I will be," Gina replied. "Pam, could you tell Bob I'm okay, so he'll give me a few minutes?"

Pam smiled and said, "Sure."

As Pam arose from the couch, Gina asked, "And do you have a few minutes?"

"I'll be right back," Pam answered. Pam exited the restroom and told Bob she was fine. He smiled in relief and walked back to his desk. Pam went back into the restroom and sat down on the couch beside Gina.

Gina asked, "Did you know Denise Steidman?" Pam shook her head. Gina stated, "She was a very nice lady who didn't deserve to be butchered!"

Pam agreed, "No, she didn't."

Gina went on, "You know it could happen to any one of us at any time. It just makes you stop and think how precious life is. It's not that I needed any reminders; I've had my share already." She paused before asking Pam, "Do you ever think about the possibility of something like that happening to you?"

Pam thought for a moment and then responded, "Like the rest of us, I'd rather see myself being killed in a blaze of glory. I don't even like to think about it, but that's a risk we take being cops."

Gina continued, "It's even more than that. Do you ever think of the risks we encounter just being females? I mean, look at the sheer number of crimes committed by men against women. It's mind boggling. Who are we supposed to trust?"

"I suppose it's just a guessing game," Pam theorized. "We trust the ones who are personable and charming. When in reality, they're probably the ones we need to keep an eye on."

Gina stated, "I have to admit. This case is really getting to me. To see my own name carved in another woman's chest as a threat, literally makes me sick. I know he's going to come after me again. Just like he said, it's only a matter of time. But I'm getting to the point I wished it would happen. Let's do it and hope for the best. I'm so angry and scared at the same time. The adrenaline rush is overwhelming. I feel I could do just about anything. I only wish I knew the identity of the man behind all of this."

Pam said, "There are rumors around the department you think John Utik is involved. Is that true?"

"Between you and me, yes. I consider him a strong suspect. But given my history with him, I can't touch him."

Gina stood up and said, "Thanks, Pam. I guess I better get back out there before Bob has a coronary." Both women smiled and then exited the restroom. They returned to find Logan on the phone and Bob in the Chief's office. Pam walked over to Logan's desk and sat down in the chair beside his desk. Gina went to her desk and called Christine. Everything was fine with her. Stan had called her a few times, but she didn't talk to him. They confirmed their plans for dinner and a movie. Gina would go by and pick her up after work.

As she hung up the phone, Bob appeared. He asked, "Do you want to talk about it, Gina?"

"No, but thanks anyway," she replied.

He suggested, "Why don't we go get a bite to eat?"

"I'm not hungry, but I'll go along for the ride."

He nodded in acknowledgment and the pair of detectives left the police station. They drove to a sandwich shop and Gina sipped on a soda, while Bob ate a huge sandwich and a bag of chips.

In between bites, Bob told her, "Talk to me. What's on your mind?"

She answered, "You won't want to hear it, but I'll tell you anyway. I was thinking about following John Utik this afternoon."

With his mouth full of chips, Bob said, "You can't be serious."

"But I am," she insisted. "Look, Bob, we don't have an abundance of suspects. Why not pursue the ones we have?"

"Because he's not an official suspect, Gina. If he was, I'm sure we'd have his attorney, Karen Rochester, breathing down our backs again for harassing him. You're playing with fire, Gina."

"That may be true," she conceded. "But I'm going to do it with or without you. I just want to follow him from a distance. There won't be any confrontation and no one will have to know about it."

Bob gulped a big drink of soda before responding. "It's against my better judgment, but okay. We'll follow him around this afternoon and see what he's up to. But promise me one thing. You won't follow him tonight or any other time without me." Gina looked away. Bob turned her chin toward him and said, "Promise me."

She hesitantly said, "Okay, I promise. Now let's get going."

They left the sandwich shop and drove to Utik's last known residence. There were two cars parked in the driveway. Gina recognized one of them, a black TransAm, as Utik's. She remembered it from the previous times she had followed him. She didn't recognize the other, a white Nissan pickup. They parked their car about a block down the street and waited. About forty-five minutes later, they saw Utik and a black man exit the house and get into their separate vehicles. They chose to follow Utik and the white Nissan sped off in the opposite direction. They followed Utik to a pawnshop on the east side. They didn't see him carry anything in. He was in the shop for about ten minutes and then got back into his car. He drove to Al's, a nearby pool hall, and went inside. They waited outside for over an hour before they saw him exit the building and get into his car. He then drove home and went into the house.

As they continued the stakeout from down the street, Bob grew more impatient. He stated sarcastically, "Well, this certainly was an eventful afternoon."

Gina said, "Look, we can leave if you want. It's getting late, anyway, and I have plans with Christine tonight."

He grinned and quickly turned the ignition on. On the way back to the station, Bob stated, "You know you have to get someone in the detective division to go with you. I'm supposed to take Lisa out for a nice dinner, but I ..."

Gina interrupted him mid-sentence, "Is it really necessary?" The look on his face said it all. "Alright, but I don't want to interrupt your dinner plans. You and Lisa have some celebrating to do. I'll ask someone else."

They arrived at the station and walked up to the detective division. Detective Logan was sitting at his desk and talking on the phone. Gina waited patiently until he hung up the phone. She then walked over to his desk.

"I'm going out tonight with a friend and the Chief insists that I have another detective following me whenever I go out off duty. Do you have plans tonight?"

"No, I don't. I can do it."

"Thank you so much. I'm sorry you have to give up your Friday night."

"Don't worry about it. I'd rather know that you're safe."

Upon hearing that, Bob wished them both a good weekend and left the station. Gina informed Logan that she was going to pick up Christine for dinner and a movie.

He asked, "So what movie are we seeing?"

"I don't know yet. I'll probably let Christine decide."

Detective Logan grabbed his jacket and they left the station in separate vehicles. When they arrived at Gina's apartment complex, Logan got out of his car and went upstairs with her. Gina unlocked her door and checked for anything out of place. She found nothing. The light on her answering machine showed no messages. With Logan waiting in the living room, she went to her bedroom and hurriedly changed into jeans and a pullover shirt. They left the apartment, got into their own cars, and drove to Christine's.

When they arrived, Logan waited in his car as Gina went into the building. She was happy to see Christine looking much better than a few days earlier. Both of her eyes were wide open and the bruises on her face were lightening in color.

Christine asked, "Are you sure we should do this? My face looks horrible."

"Of course, I'm sure," Gina replied. "It's actually looking much better. Who's going to notice in a movie theater, anyway?" Gina tried to downplay it all and added, "And we'll go to a restaurant with dim lighting. Come on."

Christine smiled and they walked downstairs to Gina's car. Gina waved at Detective Logan and told Christine he would be their escort tonight.

Christine said, "He's cute. How well do you know him?"

"Fairly well, but only at work. He seems like a really nice guy. I know that he's not married, but I don't know if he's seeing anyone." Gina was glad to hear Christine speak of someone other than Stan, even if it was just in jest.

Once they were inside the car, Gina asked, "Where would you like to eat? It's your call."

"I've really been craving Mexican food," Christine answered quickly. "How about Pedro's Cantina? I love that place!"

Gina's mind wandered to Denise Steidman. It was the same restaurant where Denise had planned to meet Valerie Bruster on the night she was killed. Gina didn't want to bring it up with Christine and make her feel like she had to choose another restaurant.

She simply said, "That sounds good."

They drove downtown to the restaurant and walked into the building. They were fortunate enough to be seated right away. It was a popular place and on a Friday night, the wait could be long. Gina noticed Logan walk into the restaurant a few minutes after them and was seated at the other side of the room.

She and Christine enjoyed a wonderful dinner; both the conversation and the food were good. Christine raved over her enchilada dinner and Gina's fajitas were delicious, too. They talked about virtually everything, from how Christine planned to stay away from Stan, to how Gina and Ted were getting along. They truly enjoyed each other's company and felt as close as sisters.

They paid for the dinner and hurried out of the restaurant. Gina let Christine decide which movie they would see. Christine had already looked at the movie listings in the newspaper and picked a romance/comedy entitled, "No more good-byes."

On the way to the theater, Gina called Detective Logan on his cell phone and told him which movie Christine had chosen. When they got there, Gina and Christine walked up to the ticket window and Detective Logan waited in his car a few minutes, so it would not appear that he was with them.

Gina and Christine sat in the middle of the theater and Detective Logan sat in the back, in order to keep a better watch over them. A few minutes later, the previews started and they nestled into their seats. After four previews, the movie began. It had a good plot, in addition to showcasing some well-known actors and actresses. It ended on a joyful note, with the couple getting back together. As expected, it was a tearjerker and left most of the women in the audience with happy tears.

Gina and Christine wiped their eyes before standing up and making their way outside. As they were almost to the car, Gina's cell phone rang. She took the phone out of her purse and recognized Bob's cell phone number on the screen.

"Yeah, Bob. What's up?"

"I need you to meet me at 3212 Cloverdale right away," he quickly answered. "It's only a couple miles from my house and I'm en route."

"What's happened?" she eagerly asked.

"There's been another homicide and from what I've been told, it looks like our guy again."

"I'll be right there."

Gina asked Detective Logan to give Christine a ride home and make sure she got into her apartment safely. She then told him to report to the Cloverdale scene. Gina and Christine gave each other a quick hug before Gina jumped into her car. She sped out of the parking lot, as Detective Logan held open the passenger door of his car for Christine.

Numerous questions flooded her mind on the way to the scene. Who would the victim be and would she know her? Would there be any messages directed at her? Would they finally catch a break and find some clues as to the murderer's identity? All of these questions, and more, would soon be answered.

CHAPTER 15

When Gina arrived at the scene, there were already several patrol cars there and the area was taped off. Neighbors stood outside in awe and dismay, hoping to catch a glimpse of what had happened. She parked her car and jogged across the street. The officer guarding the front of the house said, "Hello, Detective Perry."

She said "hello" in return and walked into the house. She was immediately greeted by Bob, who pulled her aside.

"You're not going to believe who the victim is, Gina." She stared at him inquisitively and he said, "Karen Rochester." He was right. She was taken back by it. It seemed too odd it would be John Utik's attorney. Bob continued, "There's more. I'm afraid I may owe you an apology for not taking you more seriously."

Gina asked in a confused tone, "What are you talking about?"

"Let me just show you," he said.

He led her through the living room, down the hallway, and into the master bathroom. It was a gruesome sight. On the floor in front of her, lay Karen Rochester, or at least, what was left of her. She was nude, lying face down, her entire body covered by blood. Her lower back had been ripped to shreds by a knife and her right kidney hung helplessly at her side. Her right arm was extended above her head and her index finger remained pointed on the bathroom tile. Written in blood on the tile, were the initials "J.U." Her finger remained at the top of the "U", as if death had left it there.

155

Gina turned to Bob in astonishment and he said, "Looks like you may have been right about Utik." Gina was speechless.

"They just finished taking photographs of this room and the bedroom," Bob informed. "It looks like some of the stabbing was done in there and then he finished her off in here. We can start searching the rooms for other evidence now."

As they started to walk towards the bedroom, Ralph Faraday arrived. They shook hands and showed Faraday the body. He turned her over and Gina had to turn away. Karen Rochester's abdomen and chest were literally cut open, exposing the heart, lungs, and internal organs.

Gina and Bob left Faraday to do a precursory survey of the body, while they searched for clues in the bedroom. The room was in shambles. It was apparent Rochester had struggled. Lamps lay broken, the television set was cracked, mirrors shattered, and the bed left in disarray. Her torn clothing was thrown all over the floor.

With gloves on, Gina bagged it all as evidence and Bob made an evidence log. An officer came in to dust for prints while they continued their search. They looked on the floor, in the closet, and under the bed, hoping to find something left behind. Unfortunately, they found nothing. Gina pulled the disheveled comforter off the bed, carefully folded it, and bagged it as evidence. Maybe the lab guys could find some stains or hair samples on it. She then pulled the sheets from the bed and while doing so, felt something fall on her right foot. She looked down and was amazed by what she saw. It was a pendant from a necklace. It was silver in color with serpents on the front.

"Bob, take a look at this," she said excitedly. He hurried over and she pointed to her foot. He bent down and picked it up to study it more closely. She asked, "You remember it, don't you?"

"Should I?" he replied.

With sheer enthusiasm, she said, "Yes! The last time we brought Utik in for questioning, he was wearing one just like it."

"Are you sure?" he asked.

She insisted, "Yes, I'm certain of it. I mean, I don't know if it's the exact same one, but it looked like that." Bob turned the pendant over in his hand and smiled when he saw an inscription. The word "Sly" was engraved on the back, with quotations around it.

He said, "This will help narrow it down. Do you remember this?"

"I never saw the back of it," she answered.

They both stood in silence for a moment, pondering the situation. She then exclaimed, "I have an idea! I bet he was wearing the necklace with this pendant when he was arrested. It would have been taken from him and inventoried on a property log. We could check the records and see if the inscription matches!"

"That's one hell of an idea! But first, let's see what else we can find around here."

While continuing the search in the bedroom, Gina asked, "Who found her?"

Bob reported, "Her boyfriend. She divorced last year and has been dating this guy for about 6 months. He came to pick her up for a date, but she didn't answer the door. He was worried, so he used a key she had given him to enter the front door. I already spoke with him downstairs. He seemed very credible.

She asked, "How did our guy get in?"

"He cut the screen on one of the living room windows," Bob replied.

Despite their efforts, they found no additional clues. They then walked toward the bathroom and Faraday told them he was done; the body could be bagged and taken to the morgue. Bob said, "Let's hear it, Ralph."

Faraday responded with vigor, "It appears the instrument of death was a jagged edged knife. And yes, it looks like the same kind used on the Steidman woman. I won't know for certain until I do a more thorough examination. It also appears she was raped before she was stabbed. She was probably raped in the bedroom and then killed in here."

Gina asked impatiently, "What about the initials written in blood?"

"I believe the killer left her for dead, but she survived for a short time after he left," Faraday responded. "I estimate the time of death between 7:00 and 8:00 PM. The width of the letterings match her finger, but I can't tell you with certainty right now that her fingerprints match. I have a hunch they will. I think this woman knew she was dying and wanted to tell you who did it. Do the initials mean anything to you?"

Bob stated, "There's a strong possibility."

Faraday brushed past them and said, "I'll call you when I'm through with my report."

Gina and Bob continued to search for clues throughout the house. Logan and Rogers also helped. Chief Buchanon arrived at the scene and they apprised him of what had happened. When he was told of the evidence found and its link to Utik, he looked both worried and excited.

He told them, "Look, we have to be very careful with this guy. I truly hope it is him, so we can wrap this all up. Yet, we don't want to get ourselves in hot water again. Those initials are only circumstantial and don't lead to him specifically. Perry, I want you to go down to the station right now and determine if this pendant is in fact, his. If it is, we need to get a search warrant for Utik's residence and vehicle as soon as possible."

With that, Gina said, "Wish me luck." She turned and quickly left the house. The other detectives continued the search.

The drive to the station felt like it would take forever. Gina was so excited by the possibility of the pendant belonging to Utik. She didn't really understand why he would want to kill the attorney who got him off on rape charges, but with a man like that, logical thinking didn't always apply. She finally made it to the station and hurried inside. The detective division was empty and very quiet. She began the mighty task of digging through several thick files of paperwork on John Utik. She reviewed a lot of information, but hadn't found any property logs when she reached the last file. She grew nervous at the possibility that for some reason, they hadn't been kept or were deep in storage. She thumbed through paper after paper until she found it! Included in the file was a property log dated 1/18/04 when he was arrested for receiving stolen property. She inspected the list of items taken from his person and a huge smile enveloped her face upon seeing the necklace. She couldn't help but read the description aloud, "One silver necklace with silver pendant covered by serpents, 'Sly' engraved on the back."

She immediately called Bob on his cell phone. As soon as he answered, she yelled, "It's Utik's pendant!"

Bob exclaimed, "That's wonderful news! Chief Buchanon is still here. I'll tell him about it. We're almost through and I'll see you at the station in a little while. Great job, Gina!" She thanked him and the conversation ended. She felt a great rush of satisfaction flow through her body, as she basked in the knowledge this man would finally be caught.

She decided to start writing an affidavit for a search warrant for Utik's residence and vehicle. She plugged away on the computer, detailing the evidence against him which showed probable cause for the warrant. She completed the affidavit in no time and zealously read it over to make sure she had included everything. As she was printing a copy, the elevator dinged and out stepped Chief Buchanon, Bob, Logan, and Rogers. They were all in good spirits and enthusiastically came over to Gina's desk.

Gina smiled deliriously and handed the property log to Chief Buchanon. His eyes lit up when he read the description of the pendant. He ordered, "Okay, let's type up an affidavit for a search warrant." Gina went to the printer and tore off her affidavit.

She proudly handed it to the Chief and said, "I'm open to suggestions if any of you want to change anything."

The Chief stated, "You're really on top of this, Perry. Why don't you print a few more copies and let everyone review it? Then we'll all discuss it in my office." They all nodded their heads in agreement and Chief Buchanon walked into his office. Gina printed copies for the other detectives and sat at her desk, waiting for their opinions.

Bob finished first and smiled at Gina across their desks. He commented, "I'm really proud of how you've handled this case. I know it's been rough on you, but you kept it together." Just then, Detectives Logan and Rogers approached them.

Logan asked, "Are you guys ready to go in?"

"Yes," Bob replied. All four walked into the Chief's office and sat down. The Chief started the discussion.

"You've done a good job putting this together, Perry. There are only one or two minor wording changes we need to make." He went on to tell her of those and then asked, "Does anyone else want to change anything?" They all shook their heads.

The Chief continued, "Let's make those changes and take it to a judge first thing in the morning. I'm not sure who's on the docket, but just find whoever is available and try to get him to sign off on it. In order to avoid potential problems later on, I want Logan and Rogers to present it to the judge. Logan, I want your name signed on the affidavit. Perry, your problems with this guy go way back. I don't want it to cloud the issues now. If any of you have a problem with this, I want to hear it now." No one spoke up and the Chief replied, "Good. Because it wouldn't have changed my mind, anyway." He handed the affidavit to Logan and dismissed them all.

As all four detectives left the office, Gina volunteered to Logan, "I can pull that affidavit up on my computer and help you with the changes, if you like."

"Thanks, I'd appreciate it," he responded.

They headed to her desk and in less than ten minutes, had the changes completed and a new copy printed. Logan took it in to Chief Buchanon and got final approval. All five then left the station to get some much-deserved rest.

Although Gina was exhausted both mentally and physically, she was so uptight from everything, she couldn't imagine going straight to bed. As she drove home, she passed a billboard sign that told her it was 3:30 AM. She couldn't believe it was that late. In all of the ruckus, she hadn't even glanced down at her watch. She contemplated going over to see Ted, but decided not to wake him. Tomorrow was Saturday and he would be home. She could talk to him then.

Outside her door, she saw an officer on duty. He said, "Hi. I'm Jack Winters, Officer Brooks' replacement."

Gina introduced herself and said, "Come on in. I'll get you a soda." He followed her into the apartment and helped her make certain no one else was inside. She poured two sodas and handed one to him.

They talked casually for about fifteen minutes and then he asked, "May I use your bathroom?"

"Sure," she replied.

He walked down the hallway and she heard the door close. She was glad he had been there. She felt like talking to someone and at that time of night, there weren't many people awake except cops. He came out and they wished each other a good night.

She locked the door behind him and decided to try to get some sleep; morning would come soon and tomorrow was going to be a busy day. She changed into pajamas, washed up, and crawled into bed. She stretched across the bed and set her alarm clock for 8 AM. She closed her eyes and determinedly tried not to think about the case. For if she did, she would never fall asleep.

Her alarm woke her up the next morning. She quickly got up and took a shower. She was very excited about the day and hoped it would bring closure to the case. She got dressed and had a bowl of cereal before heading out to work. She opened her door to find Officer Winters sitting in the hallway. He said, "Good morning."

She replied, "Same to you. Was it a quiet night?"

"Very," he replied groggily.

She stated, "I'm going to the station, so you can check in with your sergeant for further instructions."

Just then, Ted's door opened and she saw his smiling face. "Good morning, Ted. You're just the person I want to see."

He grinned widely and answered, "Now that's the way to start the day. How are you doing?"

She replied hopefully, "Today could be a very rewarding day."

Officer Winters stated, "I'm going to head out, if that's okay, Detective Perry."

"Sure, go ahead. I'm on my way out, too. Thanks." He walked down the hallway and stepped into the elevator. Gina and Ted continued talking in the hallway.

He asked, "Does this mean you're about to solve the case?"

She told him, "It's certainly looking that way. I'll know more after today."

He asked exuberantly, "So, how about the trip to the cabin?"

She smiled and said, "I've thought about it and would like to go with you."

His face lit up as he asked, "How about tomorrow? I have some vacation time built up. We could get away for a few days."

"Let's see how today goes," she replied. "Then I'll know if I can get any time off."

He hugged her tightly and exclaimed, "I can't wait!"

"Me, either!" she replied. "I better get going now. By the way, where are you headed on a Saturday morning? Do you have to work?"

"Yes, someone called in sick, so I'm filling in."

They walked hand in hand to the elevator and he pushed the down arrow button. They gazed at one another until they heard the elevator ding and the doors open. They stepped inside and as the doors closed, he kissed her passionately until the doors opened on the first floor. He walked her to her car and tried to open the door for her, but it was locked. She punched the button on her car alarm and it chirped twice. He then opened the door for her and she got in.

He said, "I'll call you tonight."

"Have a good day!" she replied.

He closed the door behind her and she backed out of the parking space. They waved, as she drove out of sight. Gina felt happier than she had felt for some time. She had stayed with Derick for awhile, even after their relationship began to decline. She thought it was the right thing to do at the time, but now she wondered why she hadn't ended it sooner. Not just on account of Ted, but whoever else would have made her feel this alive. She tried to look on the positive side and was thankful she hadn't stayed depressed and kept to herself any longer than she did. She would have only cheated herself from that many more wonderful days.

She arrived at the station just as Bob was pulling into the lot. They got out of their cars, exchanged pleasantries, and hurried upstairs. Logan and Rogers were nowhere to be found. Chief Buchanon came out of his office and announced, "They had an appointment with Judge Robinson at 8:30. They'll be along soon." Gina and Bob sat down at their desks and waited impatiently.

She asked him, "Why do you think Utik would want to kill his own attorney?"

"I don't know. A guy like that is hard to figure out. Maybe he came on to her during his trial and she rejected him. I don't know, Gina."

She asked, "Do you still have doubts he's the one?"

"A confession or a murder weapon would be nice," Bob answered. "But it still all points to him. Don't tell me you're having doubts!"

"I'm just exploring all the options. It surprised me that Rochester was one of the victims."

Gina thumbed through Utik's files, hoping to find some other clues. Maybe Denise Steidman was his probation officer at one time. After much review, she didn't find anything to indicate that. She stared at the wall, lost in her thoughts. Then seemingly out of nowhere, Logan and Rogers appeared.

Logan smiled and held the search warrant in front of her as he said, "We got it! Let's get ready to go in!" Gina jumped up in excitement and shook their hands; Bob did the same.

"Good work, guys!" Gina exclaimed. They all raced into the Chief's office and informed him of the results.

He was enthusiastic, "Alright, then. Let's get ready to go! Gather up the evidence collection kits and get your vests out. I'll get us some backup from the patrol division."

The four detectives quickly left the office and went to the equipment room. They gathered what they needed and told the Chief they would be outside, loading everything into their cars. He said he'd be down in a minute. They went on ahead and began piling cameras, collection kits, and other police paraphernalia into the trunks.

The Chief then came out of the building and announced, "I brought the patrol division up to speed and told them to meet us at the staging area, which I chose as the Consumer's parking lot at the corner of 12th Street and Hickory. It's only a few blocks away from Utik's residence. We'll have a couple black and whites following us out of here, but the rest are already on patrol. Let's go!" They all jumped into their cars and the parade of vehicles left the lot.

In about ten minutes, they arrived at the staging area. There were already a few patrol vehicles waiting in the parking lot. They all got out of their cars and quickly split up into teams. Each team would cover a certain side of the house, in case Utik tried to sneak out. They then devised a search plan and informed everyone of the particular evidence they were looking for in the house or car. They hoped to find the serrated hunting knife or ski mask worn during the attacks.

Once everyone understood everything, the detectives quickly put on their bulletproof vests and windbreaker jackets that had "POLICE" written in bright yellow letters on the back. They piled into their cars and drove to Utik's residence. Utik's black TransAm was parked in the driveway. Everyone bailed out of the vehicles and ran stealthily to their positions around the house. Gina stood at the edge of the front porch with her gun held out at her side, while Bob did the same at the other end. Two officers made it up to the front door and stood on each side of the doorframe. One knocked on the door and bellowed, "Police! Open up! We have a search warrant!" There was no answer. The officer knocked again, this time louder. He yelled, "Police! Open up! We have a search warrant!"

There was no sound or motion from the front of the house. Just as the two officers slammed the door with the ramming rod, they heard a lot of commotion coming from the backyard of the house. Gina heard an officer scream, "Put your hands up! Do it! You've got nowhere to go!" The officer must have gotten compliance because he then ordered, "Slowly, get down on the ground! Spread your legs!"

As Gina ran around the side of the house and swung open the wooden gate to the backyard, she saw Utik lying on the ground. Officers were handcuffing him while reading him his Miranda rights. They stood him up and his eyes met Gina's. He stared at her coldly and spit at her.

Officers and detectives had poured into the house from both directions. They methodically went through every room with weapons raised, searching for anyone else. As Gina entered the back door, she heard Bob shout, "It's all clear." They all gave a sigh of relief and an officer walked outside to Utik, with the search warrant in his hand.

The officer said for the record, "Mr. Utik, we have a warrant to search the premises."

The officer held the warrant in front of Utik's face and Utik stated calmly, "Go ahead. You won't find a thing."

"Then why'd you run?" the officer asked.

Utik glared at Gina and uttered, "Because of that bitch! She's always had it in for me and I knew she'd probably be behind all this. What's the charge this time?" She ignored him and walked back into the house. The officer sat Utik down at an old picnic table and began the vigil with another officer at his side.

The search inside began with fervor. Chief Buchanon supervised and made certain there were at least two people in every room being searched. He didn't want Utik to have the claim that any evidence found had been planted. Gina and Bob searched the living room while Logan and Rogers searched the kitchen. Officers were simultaneously searching the bedrooms, bathroom, and garage. Chief Buchanon opened the door to the garage and asked the two officers, "Have you looked in the car?"

"Not yet, sir," one replied. "But we will right now." They stumbled across the cluttered garage and manually lifted the garage door. There was so much junk in the garage there wasn't room to park the car inside.

One officer opened the driver's door of the car and began looking under the seats. The other yelled, "Pop the trunk." Chief Buchanon walked outside and watched their efforts.

The officer searching the trunk yelled, "I've got something!"

He pointed to a bloodstained towel rolled up in the corner of the trunk. The other officer brought him a camera and he took a picture of the bloody towel, exactly as it was found. With gloved hands, he picked it up and unraveled the towel in his hands. Amidst the bloody towel, lay a serrated hunting knife with about a six-inch blade, splattered with blood.

The Chief smiled and said, "Wonderful."

The officer then took more photographs of the knife. When that was done, the Chief and the two officers walked into the house and showed their find to the detectives. Their faces gleamed at the sight of it.

Bob ordered, "Package it up for the lab and I'll make out a log. Everyone else, keep looking!"

Most of the search was almost done. Everyone converged on the garage, which had the most stuff in it, but nothing was found. When that was completed, Gina asked, "Has anyone searched the yards?"

Two officers piped, "Yes, we did."

Bob gathered everyone together in the living room and asked, "Was the knife the only evidence found?"

Everyone replied, "Yes." Bob walked out the back door, with the other detectives following.

Bob told the officer, "Arrest him for the murder of Karen Rochester."

Utik stood up and screamed, "What are you talking about? Karen Rochester is my attorney, you know that!"

Bob stated, "Save the act. It's all over."

The officers began leading him out the backyard as he yelled, "What the hell's going on? Somebody killed Rochester? Why would I do that? She got me off!"

The backyard grew quiet as Utik was taken to a patrol car and driven to the station. Chief Buchanon thanked everyone for a job well done and dismissed the officers. He ordered Gina and Bob to take the knife to the lab and then report back to the station. Logan and Rogers would interrogate Utik, if he waived his right to an attorney. Otherwise, they would wait until a new attorney arrived to represent Utik. They all gathered their belongings and left the scene.

In high spirits, Gina and Bob drove to the lab. Things were looking up. They found the murder weapon in Utik's car, had his pendant at the scene, and the victim had left a dying declaration of her killer's initials in blood. He also knew the victim as his attorney. The only thing lacking was a confession, but it was doubtful they would get it. As for the murder of Denise Steidman, they would have to hope the knife matched her wounds. That homicide would be harder to prove.

While in the car, Bob asked Gina, "Did the knife look like the one used against you in your apartment?"

Gina admitted, "I couldn't say for certain because it was too dark, but it resembled it. Let's just hope the blood on the knife matches Karen Rochester's."

"Why wouldn't it?" Bob asked.

"I don't know," she replied. "Something just doesn't feel right. Why would he kill her?"

"I can't believe it!" Bob exclaimed. "You've wanted this guy all along and now that we have him, you're having doubts?"

She added, "I can't explain it. Just forget I said it."

They arrived at the lab and hurried into the building. They signed in and filled out all the necessary documents to maintain a chain of custody on the knife. They spoke briefly with a lab technician and told him they wanted the knife checked for fingerprints. They also wanted the blood analyzed to determine if it was in fact, Karen Rochester's. They told the technician the body was in the morgue and Ralph Faraday was planning to do the autopsy today. The technician said he would call them back with the results as soon as possible. They walked out of the building, got into their car, and drove to the station.

Back at the detective division, they found Logan and Rogers sitting impatiently at their desks. Bob asked, "What's going on?"

"Utik wants an attorney," Rogers replied. "We're waiting on one from the public defender's office to show up."

Logan commented, "I have to give this guy high marks for his acting ability. He really appeared shocked Rochester was dead." Everyone, but Gina, laughed.

Bob suggested, "Hey, why don't we order a couple pizzas while we're waiting. I'm starved! It will be a little while before the attorney shows up." Logan and Rogers both thought it sounded like a great idea.

Gina was lost in thought, but responded, "Sure, count me in." As the three men bickered over toppings, Gina walked over to her desk and sat down in deep contemplation.

CHAPTER 16

After about a half-hour, the pizzas arrived and they ate cheerfully. Everyone was happy with the results of the search warrant and anxiously awaited the interrogation of Utik. The Chief even came out and grabbed a slice of pepperoni pizza. He sat on the desk and said, "Bob, as senior detective, you can do the interview if you like. I know you and Perry have been working on this case the most, but I'm sorry. I don't want Perry to be a part of it. Either Logan or Rogers can sit in with you." He turned to Gina and said, "It's nothing personal. You've done a hell of a job on this. But face it, you are one of the victims and have had problems with this guy in the past. I don't know if we can even link him to the other attacks yet, but it certainly looks good on the Rochester homicide. Let's not take a chance on this, okay?"

"Yes, sir," she said.

It wasn't long before the last slice of pizza was eaten and the public defender, Ray Weston, arrived. Everyone introduced themselves and Bob showed him to the interview room. Weston explained he had already spoken with John Utik downstairs and he was ready to answer questions. Bob said, "I'll go get him." Bob walked past Logan and Rogers while saying, "Who's coming with me?"

Logan jumped in, "I will."

As Bob and Logan stepped onto the elevator, Gina, Rogers, and Chief Buchanon left the room. They walked into the room next door to the interview room, which had a one way mirror on the wall. They were all very anxious to hear what Utik had to say.

A few minutes later, Utik came into the interview room, being led by Bob and Logan. Weston stood up, as Bob sat Utik down in the chair beside Weston's. Bob and Logan then sat down across from them. Bob began, "What do you have to tell us about the murder of Karen Rochester?"

Weston interrupted, "What's your specific question, detective?" Bob took a different approach.

"We found a blood spattered hunting knife rolled up in a towel in your car. Why was it there and where did the blood come from?"

Utik was flabbergasted, "What knife? I don't know what you're talking about!"

"Do you own a hunting knife?" Bob asked.

"No, not anymore," Utik answered quickly.

Weston leaned in to Utik and whispered, "Don't volunteer anything. Just answer the question."

Bob continued, "What kind of hunting knife did you used to have?"

"Just a cheap one, nothing special," Utik said.

"What kind of a blade did it have?" asked Bob.

"It had jagged edges and was about 6 inches long. Why? You think the knife in the car belonged to me?"

"It was found in your car. Why wouldn't I think it belonged to you?" questioned Bob.

Utik exclaimed, "I haven't owned a hunting knife since last year! I'm telling you the truth! I didn't kill Karen Rochester! Why would I? She saved me from doing time last year."

Bob asked intently, "Then how would you explain the knife being in your car?"

"Maybe someone broke into my car and left it there," Utik theorized. "I don't know. Check it for fingerprints. You won't find mine on it because I had nothing to do with it."

Bob asked sarcastically, "What did you do, wipe it clean or wear gloves?"

Weston broke in, "This line of questioning is ludicrous! You're badgering my client, detective!"

Bob changed the subject, "Who calls you 'Sly'?"

Utik looked rather surprised and said, "Hardly anyone knows me by that. How did you know it was my nickname?"

"Just answer the question," Bob stated.

Weston intervened and said, "I assume there is some relevance to all of this. Get to the point."

Bob stared at Utik, who found the silence uncomfortable and answered, "Alright! It's not a big deal. My brother called me that when I was a kid because I was sneaky and always getting into trouble."

Bob inquired, "You had a pendant necklace with 'Sly' engraved on the back?"

"Yes, my brother gave it to me before he died in a car accident last year," Utik replied excitedly. "Do you know where it is? I'd really like to get it back."

Everyone watching sat in great anticipation as Bob stated, "Yes, we have it. It was found at the scene of Karen Rochester's murder." Utik sat back in his chair and rubbed his forehead with his right hand.

He then yelled, "I'm telling you I wasn't there! A couple days ago, someone jumped me in an alley. The guy took my wallet, my rings, and that necklace. I swear! It's the truth, man!"

"Did you file a police report?" Bob asked.

Utik shook his head from side to side and said, "Look, where I come from, you never go to the cops. You just cut your losses and go on."

"Do you have any proof of your story?"

"It happened when I was alone, so no," Utik answered.

Bob further questioned, "Where were you yesterday afternoon and evening?"

"At what time?" Utik asked.

"Just give me a run down of the day," Bob said.

Utik replied, "Well, I didn't do much. After lunch, I went to a pawnshop and then shot some pool with some buddies at a pool hall. Then I went home around 3:00 or 4:00 and drank some beer. I fell asleep in front of the TV and didn't wake up until early this morning." Bob knew the first part of his story was true because he and Gina had followed Utik until about 4:00. But after that, it was questionable.

Bob asked, "Did you have any friends come over?"

"No," Utik replied.

Bob plodded on, "Can anyone vouch for you being at home last night?"

"No."

Bob continued, "Did you receive any phone calls?"

Again, Utik said, "No."

Bob put it plainly, "So you have no alibi."

"No, I don't!" Utik argued. "But that doesn't mean I did it!"

Bob added, "In addition, the victim wrote your initials in blood before she died. What do you have to say about that?"

Utik was bewildered, "Look, that doesn't mean anything."

Utik's attorney broke in, "Detective, that's merely circumstantial. He's not the only person in the world with those initials. Do you have any eyewitnesses?"

"Not at this time," Bob stated firmly. "We have enough to hold him over, anyway. Mr. Weston, your client has an extensive criminal record for every crime under the sun. We found a bloodied knife of the same type used to murder Rochester in the trunk of his car. We also found a pendant at the scene, which he openly admits belongs to him. We can even prove it with a property log from one of his prior arrests. Then we have his initials etched in blood at the crime scene. And finally, he knew the victim. It would be in your client's best interests to start cooperating with us."

As Weston began whispering to Utik, the phone in the room next door began to ring. Gina picked it up and someone said, "I'm transferring a call for you, Detective Perry. It's from the lab."

"Thank you," Gina replied. She then heard the line click and she said, "Yes, this is Detective Perry."

A man's voice answered, "Yes, this is Joe from the lab. I spoke with you this morning in reference to the knife."

Gina said, "Yes, Joe. What did you find out?"

He explained, "First of all, there were no prints on the knife. Secondly, I went over to talk with Ralph Faraday, but he wasn't there.

It turns out he's at home sick with a really bad flu. So your autopsy on Rochester hasn't been done. I'm still waiting for the blood and DNA comparisons between Utik and Rochester. I'll let you know when I get the results.

"Thanks, Joe," Gina said.

She relayed the results to the others in the room and Chief Buchanon told Detective Rogers to tell Bob. Rogers got up and walked to the interview room. He knocked on the door and Bob yelled, "Come on in!" Utik and his attorney were still whispering to one another, while Bob and Logan sat quietly. Rogers walked over to Bob, bent down, and whispered the details of the phone conversation with the lab. Bob stared directly at Utik, as Rogers left and returned to the room next door.

Utik and Weston finally stopped conversing and Bob asked, "Would you like to change your story?" Utik looked at his attorney, but said nothing. Gina realized Bob was trying to bluff Utik into thinking they had received further evidence against Utik.

Bob stated smugly, "Look, you're in serious trouble here. Not only are you directly connected to the murder of Karen Rochester, but possibly other attacks against women." Utik's face turned pale as Bob continued, "Since Shirley Jenson was raped and beaten, there have been other rapes in which the assailant used the same type of weapon. The physical description was also the same."

Weston interrupted, "You're out of line. My client was found not guilty of the Jenson rape and therefore, how can you tie him in to the others?"

Bob answered in a cocky manner, "For starters, the knife found in his car is of the same type as the one used in other attacks, one of which was the murder of Denise Steidman. I'll bet the wounds on the victims would narrow it down even further." Bob then looked at Weston with a serious look on his face.

Bob said, "There's something else. There was an attack against my partner, Detective Perry, last week. A man broke into her apartment and held a knife to her throat. I should add the description of the knife fits the one used most recently. Fortunately, the attack was interrupted, but she has been continually harassed since then. Mr. Weston, your client has threatened my partner on numerous prior occasions. Things do not look good for him right now."

Weston stated, "My client has nothing more to say at this time."

Utik screamed, "Yes, I do!" Against the advice of his attorney, Utik said, "I'm not going to do time for something I didn't do. Yes, it's true I threatened Perry in the past, but I didn't break into her apartment and I haven't been harassing her! You mentioned some woman by the name of Steidman who was murdered; I don't even know who she is. Look, I know I'm not the smartest guy on the block, but I know a little bit about the law. I know I can't be tried twice for the same crime. I didn't commit these rapes and murders you're talking about. I will admit this now to show you I'm being straight with you. I did rape Shirley Jenson last year."

Everyone sat in silence, shocked he would admit it after all this time. Utik continued, "That trial really made me think about things. I never thought about how it affected a woman until I heard her on the stand. I'm not saying I've been an angel, but I haven't harmed any women since then. You gotta believe me!" His eyes stared pleadingly at Bob and Logan. Then he said, "And as for the knife you found in my car, why would I tell you to go ahead and search everything if I knew it was in my car? That would be stupid!"

Bob commented, "We had a search warrant in hand. It wouldn't have mattered what you told us."

Ray Weston stood up and said to Utik, "You'll probably go before the magistrate on Monday. I'll review the case and be in touch."

"That's it?" Utik exclaimed. "You mean I have to stay in jail?"

"I'm afraid so," Weston replied.

Weston then knelt down and whispered something in Utik's left ear. No one knew what was said, but Utik became silent. Weston shook everyone's hands and left a couple business cards on the table, before exiting the room. Bob turned towards the mirror and smiled; it was obvious he was ecstatic. Bob and Logan then led Utik out of the room and took him downstairs to the jail.

Chief Buchanon was thrilled. He turned to Gina and exclaimed, "I think we've got our man!" Rogers echoed the same opinion. All three left the room and waited for the return of Bob and Logan in the detective division. A few moments later, they arrived, grinning from ear to ear.

Bob stated with relief, "Well, I think it's finally over. Can you believe some of the things he said? That someone jumped him in an alley a few days ago and stole his pendant necklace? And the one about someone breaking into his car and leaving the knife? He was really grasping."

"I guess it's not that far-fetched coming from him," Logan added. "What did we expect, a confession?"

"I want to congratulate all of you for your hard work on this case," the Chief stated. "But it's not over. We have a lot of circumstantial evidence. It would be nice to find an eyewitness or a friend of his who he bragged to about the crimes. That would definitely seal his fate, if we haven't already. Perry, I want you to take a couple days off effective immediately. This whole thing has been harder on you than any of us. Take some time and get away from it. There will be plenty to do on it when you get back."

Gina replied, "But what about the autopsy results and...?"

The Chief stopped her mid-sentence, "One of these gentlemen can handle it." She knew he was serious, so she dropped the subject.

The Chief told everyone they were free to go. He walked to his office and got on the phone. Logan and Rogers immediately grabbed their jackets and left the station. Bob walked down the hall to the restroom, as Gina sat down at her desk. She stared at the wall until Bob returned and asked, "Why are you still here? You heard what the Chief said. You're on vacation. I'll call Faraday and see when he plans to do the autopsy. Hopefully, we'll hear back from the lab soon that the blood on the knife matches Karen Rochester's. I can handle things here. You take the time off and enjoy yourself."

"It all seems too neat," she softly stated.

"What are you talking about?" Bob asked.

"This whole case," she answered. "For a week, we can't put anything together and then all of a sudden, we have evidence galore. I just think it all fits together too simply. I know you'll think I'm crazy for saying this, but part of me believed Utik. Why would he want to kill Rochester, the one person who saved him from spending years in prison?"

Bob laughed and said, "You're right. I do think you're crazy. You've wanted to nail this guy for a long time and now that we have him, you think he's telling the truth? Gina, you do need a vacation! Besides, he admitted to us he raped Jenson. Maybe he admitted this to Rochester during the trial. True, she couldn't do anything with that knowledge due to attorney-client privileges, but maybe she inadvertently said or did something which showed her genuine disgust of him. Then he waits awhile after the trial before he kills her. That way, everyone would wonder just what you're thinking. Why would he kill the attorney who got him off?"

"I guess you're right, Bob," Gina conceded. "I'm just exhausted from all of this."

"What do you plan to do with your time off?" he asked. She smiled gleefully, recalling Ted's invitation to the cabin at the lake.

"I'm going to 'The Water's Edge' with Ted," she answered.

Bob said, "I went there once years ago. It's beautiful and very secluded. It would be a good place for you to relax and forget about Utik."

"You're absolutely right!" Gina enthused. "As of now, my thoughts are going to be tuned in on better things!" She grabbed her purse from the desk and started to walk away. She turned back and gave him a big hug while saying, "Thank you so much for everything, Bob! I'll call you when I get back."

"Have a good time and take care," he said. She then left the station and all thoughts of it.

She quickly drove home and hurried into the building. She knocked on Ted's door, but he wasn't home. She found it very refreshing that there was no longer an officer standing watch in the hallway. She could finally resume her personal life and do whatever she pleased. It had been awhile since she went away for a few days, let alone with a man like Ted. She unlocked her door and went inside, locking it behind her. She checked her answering machine and saw she had two messages. She pushed the play button and listened. The first was from Christine, asking Gina to call her back as soon as she got in. The second was from Ted. He had gotten home from work earlier, but had run out to do some errands. He said he would stop by when he got back.

She called Christine and it only rang once before Christine picked up and said, "Hello."

"Hi," Gina replied. "I'm sorry I had to leave you last night."

Christine laughed and said, "Well, I'm not. Detective Logan asked me out! He's really nice, Gina. We're going out tonight. Can you believe it? He doesn't mind taking out a woman with bruises on her face!"

"I'm happy for you," Gina replied. "I have news to share, too. We have Utik in custody and believe he's our man. The Chief told me to take some time off, so Ted and I are going to a cabin at 'The Water's Edge' tomorrow."

Christine shouted, "That's wonderful, Gina! It's about time you put Derick behind you and move on with your life. When are you leaving?"

"Probably in the morning," Gina answered. "I'm really looking forward to it! Listen, I don't want to hold you up. Have a good time tonight. I'll call you when I get back."

"You have a good time, too. Bye."

"Good-bye," Gina said, and hung up the phone.

She flitted to her bedroom closet and pulled out a suitcase from the top shelf. She threw it on the bed and joyfully began filling it with casual clothes. She heard a knock at the door and hurried to the peephole, to find Ted waiting in the hall. She quickly unlocked the door and let him in. "I have something to show you," she said.

"I like the sound of that," he replied. She grabbed his hand and led him to her bedroom to see her suitcase stuffed with clothes.

"Does this mean what I think it means?" he asked.

"Yes!" she squealed. "Let's leave in the morning!"

He picked her up and swung her around while saying, "That's great, Gina! I was keeping my fingers crossed all day in the hopes we could go away together."

He put her down and kissed her gently. "I have to go make some calls to my boss and my friend who owns the cabin," he said. "What are your plans tonight?"

"I need to finish packing," she replied. "Maybe we could order some take-out for dinner. I'm really excited right now, but I know I'm so tired I'm going to crash soon. I'd like to go to bed early and get a good night's sleep for tomorrow."

"Why don't I go make those calls now?" he suggested. "Do you mind running out for some Chinese food or something?"

"No," she answered. "That sounds like a good idea. What would you like?"

"Oh, cashew chicken sounds good," he responded. He pulled out his wallet and handed her a twenty dollar bill. "It's my treat." She accepted the twenty and grabbed her purse, before they both exited her apartment. He went into his apartment and she walked down the hall to the elevator.

She got into her car and drove to a Chinese restaurant a few blocks away. She placed their orders and it was ready in a short time. She walked back to her car and placed the hot bag on the passenger seat. The scrumptious aroma permeated the car the whole way home. She opened the apartment door to find Ted engrossed in a phone conversation. She went into the kitchen and began emptying the take-out containers onto plates. He ended his conversation and walked into the kitchen.

"It smells great," he said. He opened the refrigerator and took out some sodas. While popping the tops, he said excitedly, "It's all set! My boss gave me a couple days off and the cabin is all ours!"

She gave him a big hug and said, "Thank you. You don't know how much I need some time away."

They carried their plates and sodas to the table and sat down. They ate their dinner happily, as he told her about the cabin and things they could do, such as hiking, fishing, and canoeing. After dinner, Ted said, "You should go get some sleep. I'm going to run over to my friend's house to pick up the keys and then I'll go to the store to get some groceries." She offered to go with him, but he could see how tired she was and told her that he would take care of it. They parted in the hallway with a long kiss and she went into her apartment.

Deep down, she was glad he didn't want her to go with him. She was exhausted, both mentally and physically. She packed a little bit more and decided she would finish up in the morning. She changed into pajamas and moved her suitcase from the bed to the floor. She crawled into bed and snuggled underneath the covers. The coolness made her recall Ted telling her it would be cooler at the lake and she should bring warm clothes. She looked forward to tomorrow evening, when she would be cuddling with Ted near a roaring fire. For the first time in over a week, she fell asleep quickly, with a smile on her face.

CHAPTER 17

Next morning, she jumped out of bed and pulled up the blinds on the bedroom window. It was a gorgeous day. The sun was shining boldly and a gentle breeze blew the leaves on the trees. After a relaxing shower, she changed into a pair of jeans and a flannel shirt. As she was combing out her hair, she heard a knock at the door. She unlocked the door and let Ted in. He was wearing jeans, a long sleeved pullover shirt, and hiking boots.

"Good morning," he said. "How long do you need before you're ready to go?"

"Oh, about twenty minutes."

He smiled and said, "I'll start loading the Explorer." They parted and she hurriedly finished getting ready.

She helped him finish loading the vehicle and they pulled out of the parking lot at 9:30 AM. The drive up to the cabin seemed to fly by, as they talked non-stop. They arrived at the cabin shortly before noon. Gina hopped out of the car and stood in awe of the scenery. The lake, nestled in pines, was huge and its water sparkled in the sunlight. Squirrels ran amuck. The cabin looked as rustic as she had imagined, but it also looked very well kept. Ted took her hand and led her to the cabin saying, "Let me show you the place." He unlocked the front door and said, "I know it's small, but it's cozy." She looked around and saw a tiny kitchen and a quaint living room area. It had a couch, two recliners, and a nice fireplace. He led her down a short hallway and said, "Yes, it has indoor plumbing." On the right, was a small bathroom and on the left, the bedroom.

"This place is just perfect," she said.

They walked outside and headed toward the lake, which wasn't far from the cabin. He showed her to a small outbuilding which had a canoe turned upside down beside it. He opened the door and said, "This is where all the tools and fishing gear are kept." She stepped inside and saw everything from fishing poles, to shovels, to an axe propped up against the wall. She stepped back outside and looked across the lake to the far shore, which was a long distance away.

She could vaguely make out some houses and asked, "Is the other side more populated?"

"Yes," he answered. "My buddy owns several acres on this side. That's why there are no other houses nearby. His father bought this property a long time ago, before it was ever popular. His father passed away and he got this in the inheritance."

They walked back up to the car and began unloading their things. Shortly thereafter, everything was safely in the cabin. They ate some cheese and crackers for a snack and then decided to go for a hike in the woods. Before they left, she took her 9-millimeter from her purse and tucked it into the back of her waistband. She pulled her flannel shirt out to conceal it. She knew she was off duty and on vacation in the woods, but couldn't convince herself she didn't need it with her. She hurried outside, to where Ted was waiting patiently. They walked hand in hand, exploring the area around the cabin. They never passed any other houses, even though they covered quite a distance. The scenery was simply magnificent and its peacefulness had a calming effect on Gina. She began to feel at ease; past troubles seemed to drift out of her mind and body.

They sat down on a log near the water and kissed. "Thank you for bringing me here," she said.

"The pleasure is all mine," he answered. "I can't think of anyone else I would rather be here with, Gina. I know we haven't known each other very long, but you mean a lot to me."

"And you mean a lot to me," she added. "You really came along at a good time. Sometimes, it's hard for me to admit I need people, but I do. I need you in my life."

He leaned down and kissed her passionately, while he guided her body from the log to the ground and covered her body with his own. She felt his tongue in her mouth, as his body pressed firmly against hers. She kissed him back energetically for a moment, but then stopped. Their lips parted and he asked, "What's wrong?"

She laughed as she said, "This gun's killing my back!" He arose to his knees, allowing her to remove the gun from the small of her back. She said, "I guess I don't need this out here." It was not only its physical presence getting in the way, but also the way it made her feel emotionally. She was ready to open her soul to this man and follow her heart. At that moment, she was just someone in the woods, not a cop. She needed to allow herself that carefree independence and let all barriers down.

She suggested, "Why don't we go back to the cabin and drop my gun off there? Then we could take the canoe out and go fishing."

Ted looked a bit surprised, but said, "Okay."

She kissed him softly and then whispered in his ear, "We have all night." His smile returned and they hiked back to the cabin.

"I'll wait out here," he said, as she ran into the cabin. She placed her gun in the nightstand beside the bed and then used the bathroom. She hurried outside and helped Ted carry the canoe and fishing gear down to the lake. They set the canoe down in the water and got in. With Ted doing most of the paddling from the back, they glided out to deeper waters. A short time later, they found a quiet cove and cast their lines.

They fished for a couple of hours at different locations. Gina caught three smallmouth bass to his one bluegill. Neither liked fish much, so they released them. They both paddled back to the cabin, as she joked with him about the size of his fish. They pulled the canoe ashore and carried the gear back to the shed. He suggested, "Why don't we grill some burgers outside before it gets dark? I'll start the grill."

"That sounds great!" she replied. "I'll go make the patties and bring them out."

"I'll also chop some wood for tonight while you're doing that," he added. "I noticed there were only a couple logs at the fireplace." She went into the cabin and began making the hamburgers.

While doing so, she heard the sound of Ted chopping wood outside. It was a calming sound, one she didn't hear often. She loved being in the wilderness and knew she would have difficulty going back to the hustle-bustle of city life. But she would worry about it later, not now. Her happiness would not be interrupted tonight. She would not allow that to happen.

She took out the burgers and put them on the grill, as Ted continued to chop wood with the axe from the shed. It was getting cooler outside, as the sun began to set behind the trees. She rushed back inside and began setting the table for dinner.

About ten minutes later, Ted came inside with the cooked burgers. He commented on how chilly it had become and handed her the plate of hamburgers. He tended to the fireplace and started a fire with the logs left in the cabin.

"I'll bring more wood in after dinner," he said. She filled the table with condiments for the burgers, then chips, and then their drinks. The fire began to crackle, as Ted stood up and walked to the kitchen to wash his hands.

Gina commended him, "These burgers look great! We really worked up an appetite today." He smiled and nodded his head in agreement.

He pulled out a bag from a kitchen drawer and took out two white candles. He placed them in holders and set them down on the table. He then dimmed the lights, lit the candles, and sat down. He said, "I know this isn't a fancy meal or anything, but you can make anything romantic with the right person." She smiled and kissed him gently across the table. They enjoyed a cozy meal and wonderful conversation, while Gina secretly fantasized how the evening would progress.

They finished eating and quickly cleaned up the kitchen. Ted didn't know if she was quite ready to go to bed yet and he didn't want to seem over-eager. "Would you like to make some s'mores from the remaining fire outside?" he asked. She walked up to him, grabbed his shirt, and pulled him towards her.

"I'd rather do this," she said, as she kissed him feverishly. He picked her up and began to carry her to the bedroom. He was surprised to hear her say, "Wait a minute." He looked at her sincerely, confused by her actions. She asked, "Wouldn't it be better out here in front of the roaring fire? Do you have some blankets we could lay down on the floor?"

He put her down quickly and excitedly remarked, "I'm sure I can find some." She used the bathroom while he found some blankets and laid them out on the floor in front of the fireplace.

She returned and laid down on the floor beside him. They gazed into one another's eyes and his lips sought hers. They rolled playfully on the blankets and stopped with Ted atop her, kissing her wildly. He unbuttoned her shirt, just as the flames from the fire disappeared. The room was dark, except for the dim light of the candles on the table. They both stopped and he said, "Damn, I forgot to bring the firewood in!" They both laughed, as they looked at the empty woodbin at the edge of the fireplace.

"Would you please get some more wood?" she asked.

He sighed and said, "Sure, Gina. Just hold that thought!"

"You should bring a big armful," she replied flirtatiously. "You're going to be busy for quite awhile." He grinned and walked out of the cabin.

Gina rolled onto her stomach and dreamily stared at the embers in the fireplace until she heard the door open and close. A rush of cool air had blown in, leaving goosebumps on her body. She closed her eyes, in anticipation of Ted's touch. She heard him walking slowly towards her and then felt him straddle her waist. He began rubbing her shoulders and she moaned in pleasure. But then she opened her eyes, noting she hadn't heard him drop the wood at the fireplace. The room was only dimly lit by the distant candles. She turned her head around to ask Ted about the fire. Her body jerked at the sight of the figure straddling her body. He carefully rolled her over so he could better see her face. He remained straddling her waist and peered down at her, while holding her trembling hands above her head.

Gina's breathing became very labored by what she saw before her. The person atop her was wearing a black ski mask and she felt fabric against her wrists from the gloves he was wearing. It looked like the same ski mask worn by the attacker in her apartment. Her skin crawled. Who was on top of her? She didn't know. She couldn't bring herself to believe Ted could be involved. This person was wearing different clothing, but that didn't prove anything.

She pleaded, "Just let me see your face!"

The man laughed and said, "You still don't know who I am. Let's just say I've watched you for a long time." His voice sounded somewhat familiar, but she couldn't seem to place it.

"What do you want from me?" she asked.

"Everything you represent," he replied.

She felt his grip loosening around her wrists, as he spoke with confidence. She jerked her right hand free and grabbed at his mask before he could stop her. As she pulled it from his head, he regained control and clinched her hand which held the mask tightly.

She couldn't believe her own eyes. She could now see him clearly, as the light of the candles shone on his crazed face. A devilish grin formed, leaving his teeth to sparkle brightly. His eyes beamed in celebration of this long awaited moment. She lay there stunned, her body paralyzed by fear and shock.

He sarcastically stated, "Detective Perry, I do believe this is the first time I've seen you speechless."

She screamed, "Judge Slocum, you pompous asshole! It's been you all along?" He laughed loudly, but said nothing. She gathered her composure and stated, "You have nothing to lose by telling me all about it. I know you're dying to brag. You're going to kill me anyway, right?"

"Yes, but not for awhile," he answered. "We're going to have some fun first. What's it matter to you? You were just about to give it to that bum outside. Just pretend I'm him."

He leaned down to kiss her, but she spit in his face. She yelled, "What did you do with Ted?" He pinned her down tightly while he leaned down and wiped his face on her gaping shirt.

He then stared directly into her tearful eyes and said, "I hit him over the head with a rock. He wasn't moving, so don't think your Romeo is going to burst in here and save the day." She whimpered, but continued asking Judge Slocum questions. She had an intense desire to learn more, whether she was to live or die on this beautiful night in the wilderness.

"How did you know I was here?" she asked.

"I overheard you talking to your partner in the parking lot after Steidman's funeral," he responded. "It wasn't difficult to locate you up here."

She reflected on that day and said, "I remember telling Bob I was going to come up here when things settled down, but I didn't say when because I didn't know."

He grinned and said, "That's why I had to give you John Utik on a silver platter. He was my scapegoat all along." He apparently then got tired of holding her hands down to the floor, so he pulled her arms down and pinned them between his legs and her body. He smiled and said, "You're right. I am thoroughly enjoying telling you all of this. You should feel honored. I didn't tell the others very much. But you're special to me. I have planned for you the longest. You have been a great challenge to me and for that, I applaud you. But you deserve to die, just like those other bitches who forgot they were women and tried to act like men!"

Gina led him on by saying, "Tell me about it." He jumped on the opportunity.

"You all strut into my courtroom wearing those skirts, silk blouses, and sweet perfume, with the notion that you, mere women, can make a difference. You pull that idealistic bullshit on juries and come out smelling like a rose. It's my courtroom; you're simply a guest in it. My word goes!" She said nothing, anxiously waiting for him to continue, which he did momentarily. "Don't you understand? Women were not meant to be cops, probation officers, attorneys, or firefighters. Those are positions to be held by men, who are better able to make important decisions. Women have no business holding those jobs. It leaves less for men and gives women more power than they should have."

"What made you start to think that way?" Gina asked.

"My father was a great man, a mechanic by trade," he answered. "He treated my mother very well, but she was never satisfied. She didn't comprehend her true purpose in life. She was a sergeant in the Army and spent most of her time at work, leaving my father to take care of me. She made a lot more money than he did and she made him feel inadequate. She ordered us around and treated us like subordinates. My father couldn't take it anymore and killed himself. It wasn't long after, my mother had an accident in the car."

He smiled deviously and Gina gasped in dismay, "You killed her?"

He calmly stated, "I knew then it was up to me to provide true justice. She deserved to die. Her actions killed her; I just tampered with the brakes and put her out of her misery. My father would have thanked me."

Gina sighed and he asked her, "What else do you want to know before I torture you? Don't think this little conversation will make me spare you. I've waited for this for a long time and plan to enjoy myself. We have all the time in the world."

"How did Utik become a part of this?" she asked.

He spoke with cockiness, "That was the easy part. I knew you despised him and would hunt him down like an animal. Hell, you later proved that by disobeying my direct orders to stay away from him. When he was on trial for the Jenson rape, I noticed we were about the same size. I knew everyone thought he was guilty; so did I. But I thought he would serve me better on the outside. Therefore, I allowed Rochester a lot of leeway and helped set him free. Then I dressed like him and used a knife just like the one presented in court. I knew you would think it was him. I scared the firefighter so badly she wouldn't even press charges. I had thought about killing her, but just didn't feel like it that night. After I killed Steidman, it came easy. I really wanted you next, but you were always guarded. So I figured if I handed you Utik, you would let your guard down again."

"What about the knife found in Utik's car?" she asked.

"That's simple. I just broke into the trunk and left it there for you to find."

"And the pendant from his necklace?" she asked.

"That required a little more work," he admitted. "I paid a thug off the street to jump him and make it look like a robbery. When the guy gave me the pendant, I knifed him in the chest and dumped the body down a sewage drain. He'll turn up eventually with Utik's wallet in his pocket. After I did Rochester, I left the pendant there for you. I knew you would recognize it because he had worn it in court."

"And the initials 'J.U.' left in blood by Rochester?"

Judge Slocum roared, "That's news to me! I thought the bitch was dead when I left her in the bathroom. She must have been trying to write 'JUDGE,' but died before she finished. And of course, you stupid cops assumed it meant John Utik. That's hilarious! I couldn't have planned it better myself!"

He continued to laugh uncontrollably as Gina's blood boiled within her. She had heard enough and her focus turned to methods of escape. If she could only make it to the bedroom, she could grab her gun from the nightstand. She eyed the poker near the fireplace and saw he was so caught up in himself, he wasn't paying much attention. His legs were not pinning her arms very tightly, as he rocked back and forth howling in laughter. She thrust her right hand free and pushed him off balance. She leaned towards the fireplace and grabbed the poker. She hit him in the head with the poker and he fell to the floor, blood dripping from the left side of his face. She kicked him off of her and he grabbed one of her legs as she started towards the bedroom. She raised the poker again and slammed it down on his hand. She heard crackling that sounded like bones had been broken, as he let go and screamed in agony.

"You bitch! You're not going to get away with this!"

She ran to the bedroom and snatched her 9-millimeter from the nightstand. She dropped the poker down on the bed and began walking down the hallway, with her weapon raised. She could feel her hands shaking against the cool metal of the weapon. Her heart raced, as she slowly maneuvered her way toward evil.

She rounded the corner and saw him standing in front of the fireplace, holding his left hand, the one she had hit with the poker. She closed the distance between them quickly, while ordering him to put his hands up. He only laughed at her and stepped towards her. She yelled, "You take one more step and you're dead!"

Undaunted, he stepped forward. She pulled the trigger, but nothing happened. She tried again and again, but the magazine was empty. He knocked the weapon out of her hand and shoved her against the wall, while laughing hysterically.

He told her, "I watched you out in the woods this afternoon and heard you say that you planned to leave your gun in the cabin.

When you went fishing, I emptied the clip. But don't worry. I don't plan to use it on you. It's not my style. Slow deaths are much more gratifying."

She kneed him in the groin and he fell to the floor in agony. She threw the door open and ran outside. She desperately searched around the cabin, but didn't see Ted anywhere. She spotted the axe, propped up against a log, and grabbed it with both hands. By the light of the full moon, she ran down the path to the lake. She threw the axe into the canoe and began frantically pushing the canoe off shore. She jumped in and began swiftly paddling out onto the lake. She heard the door of the cabin slam shut, but kept going. Then his voice roared across the lake, amidst the fog that had quickly rolled in.

"I'll kill him, Gina! You come back right now or I'll cut his throat!"

She stopped paddling and looked back to the cabin on the hill. She could only see one obscured figure through the fog and darkness. The figure stood amidst the trees, about halfway between the cabin and the shore.

Gina called out, "Come out where I can see you!" He stepped out into the moonlight, dragging Ted with him.

She yelled, "How do I even know he's still alive?"

"Come in closer and I'll prove it to you!" he shouted.

She paddled to within about thirty yards of the shore, as Judge Slocum dragged Ted near the water's edge. When she stopped paddling, he kicked Ted in the stomach. Ted clutched his ribs and groaned.

Obviously, she couldn't leave without Ted. Although he was alive, he was incapable of defending himself due to the blow to his head. She took a deep breath and began paddling towards the shore. When she neared land, Judge Slocum ordered her, "Throw both paddles in the water. I know how your mind works, Gina. You're not going to hit me with those damn things!"

She tossed the paddles into the water and drifted to the shoreline, where he stood waiting. He grabbed the front of the canoe and began pulling it ashore. With both hands, she clutched the axe on the floor of the canoe. As he came closer, she suddenly raised the axe and struck his shins. The force of the blow caused him to fall backward on land, giving her time to jump out of the canoe on the other side and get to Ted, who was lying unconscious less than ten feet away.

In a maddened frenzy, Judge Slocum stood up, oblivious to the pain. He wielded a hunting knife and spouted off, "I must destroy you and all those like you! As judge, I hereby sentence you to death!"

He charged towards her and she swung the axe instinctively. It landed on his right arm, knocking the knife to the ground. Blood gushed from his arm, as the axe had cut halfway through.

He eyed the knife on the ground between them and Gina yelled, "It's over! Step away from the knife!"

He grinned and said, "It will never be over. I will always live on in your mind."

She held the axe above her right shoulder and again yelled, "Step away from the knife!"

He lunged for it and she slammed the axe into the left side of his head, knocking him backwards. A loud splash was heard, as the sinister one fell lifelessly into the cool waters. Justice was served, by the Dishonorable Judge William Slocum subsiding.

About the Author

Vicki Lucky was born in Connecticut, but grew up primarily in Missouri. She always had a passion for mysteries and the investigative field.

She graduated from Missouri Southern State College with a Bachelor of Science in Criminal Justice Administration and Associate of Science in Law Enforcement in 1991.

She has worked as an investigator of various types for the last fifteen years, including as a background investigator for the federal government, a federal criminal investigator, and currently a private investigative contractor.

She lives in a small town in southern Missouri.

Printed in the United States
86649LV00008B/229-231/A